LARA

British-Nigerian writer Bernardine Evaristo is the award-winning author of eight books and numerous other published and produced works that span the genres of novels, poetry, verse fiction, short fiction, essays, literary criticism, and radio and theatre drama. Her latest novel, *Girl, Woman, Other* (Hamish Hamilton/Penguin, 2019), was joint winner with Margaret Atwood's *The Testaments* of the 2019 Booker Prize for Fiction.

Her other books include: *Mr Loverman* (Hamish Hamilton/ Penguin, 2013), about a 74-year-old Caribbean London man who is closet homosexual; *Hello Mum* (Penguin, 2010), an epistolary novella about gang culture; *Lara*, an earlier version of which was published by Angela Royal in 1997, and which Evaristo rewrote and expanded by a third for its new edition (2009) from Bloodaxe Books; *Blonde Roots* (Penguin, 2008), her first prose novel, featuring an alternate universe in which Africans enslave Europeans; *Soul Tourists* (Penguin, 2005), a novel-with-verse, which features ghosts of colour from European history including Pushkin, Shakespeare's 'Dark Lady of the Sonnets' and Alessandro dei Medici; and *The Emperor's Babe* (Penguin, 2001), a verse novel about a black girl growing up in Roman London nearly 2000 years ago.

She co-edited a special issue of *Wasafiri* magazine, *Black Britain: Beyond Definition* (2010), which celebrated and reevalu- ated the black writing scene in Britain, and was guest editor of of *Poetry Review*, with her issue, *Offending Frequencies* (2012), featuring more poets of colour than had previously been pub- lished in a single issue of the journal. In 2012 she was Chair of both the Caine Prize for African Fiction and the Commonwealth Short Story Prize. She has won several awards and her books have been a 'Book of the Year' twelve times in British newspapers. She joined the governing Council of the Royal Society of Liter ature in 2016 and became Vice Chair in 2017. She was awarded an MBE in 2009.

BERNARDINE EVARISTO

LARA

'the family is like water'

BLOODAXE BOOKS

ISBN: 978 1 85224 831 4

New edition published 2009 by
Bloodaxe Books Ltd,
Eastburn,
South Park,
Hexham,
Northumberland NE46 1BS.

Original edition published in 1997
by Angela Royal Publishing.

Reprinted 2010, 2013, 2017, 2019

www.bloodaxebooks.com
For further information about Bloodaxe titles
please visit our website and join our mailing list
or write to the above address for a catalogue

Supported by
**ARTS COUNCIL
ENGLAND**

Cover design: Neil Astley & Pamela Robertson-Pearce

Printed in Great Britain by Bell & Bain Limited, Glasgow, Scotland, on
acid-free paper sourced from mills with FSC chain of custody certification.

For Jack (Obayomi), Charlie (Oladimeji),
Natasha (Iyabo) and Marlon (Akinola)
Inheritors of this history...

LARA DA COSTA FAMILY TREE

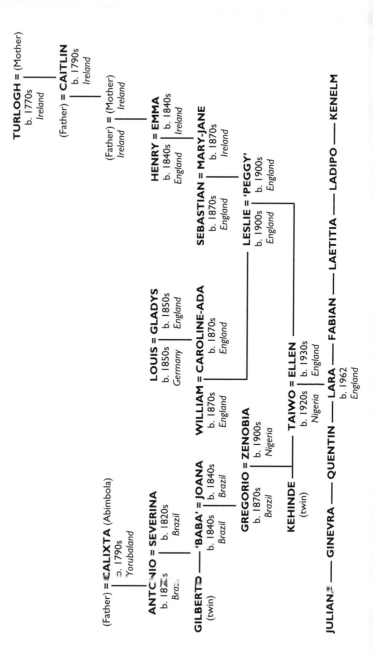

TURLOGH = (Mother)
b. 1770s
Ireland

CAITLIN
b. 1790s
Ireland

(Father) = (Mother)
Ireland | Ireland

HENRY = EMMA
b. 1840s | b. 1840s
England | Ireland

SEBASTIAN = MARY-JANE
b. 1870s | b. 1870s
England | Ireland

LESLIE = 'PEGGY'
b. 1900s | b. 1900s
England | England

LOUIS = GLADYS
b. 1850s | b. 1850s
Germany | England

WILLIAM = CAROLINE-ADA
b. 1870s | b. 1870s
England | England

(Father) = CALIXTA (Abimbola)
d. 1790s
Yorubaland

ANTONIO = SEVERINA
b. 182?s | b. 1820s
Bra?i? | Brazil

GILBERTO —— 'BABA' = JOANA
b. 1840s | b. 1840s
(twin) Brazil | Brazil

GREGORIO = ZENOBIA
b. 1870s | b. 1900s
Brazil | Nigeria

KEHINDE —— TAIWO = ELLEN
(twin) | b. 1920s | b. 1930s
Nigeria | England

JULIAN —— GINEVRA —— QUENTIN —— LARA —— FABIAN —— LAETITIA —— LADIPO —— KENELM
b. 1962
England

However far the stream flows,
it never forgets its source

YORUBA PROVERB

INDEX OF FIRST LINES

Part One

Part Two

PART ONE

PROLOGUE

SUGAR CANE, damp musky earth, saccharine vanilla
journeys in from Eighteen Forty-Nine, scenting Lara.
Disembodied chords pluck the air.
                                    'Severina
- the scarred one. They took me while my boys slept,
my bones had shivered all day, I could barely think.
When I bent to work I imagined vultures clawing
my back. When his men came I heard my bones jangle
like wooden sticks shaking in a bowl. His chamber,
sunk in the cellars of that great house, kept for us
women, only. There he pierced me with a bayonet
as I lay on a marble slab, bound. My screams
ricocheted the walls, he ejaculated on my ruptured
body but by then I had become the fire of a naked torch,
until he put me out. Then I jumped a spider,
crept deftly through the warren of cellars into daylight
where a bird swooped me up. I became that bird,
circled the fazenda until a baobab seed rooted
from my droppings. When it broke through earth
into life, I lived in that tree, grew quickly, saw one
of my seeds planted by my stronger son over my husband
Antonio's dead body, and so it continued. I was carried over
the ocean, burst into life, watched over Baba until
he joined us nearly a century after my death.
                                    So you have it.'

CHAPTER 1

TAIWO

OH MAMA! Your pride when I boarded the *Apapa*.
Your son, a man now, riding the whale to paradise.

Remember the man's voice from Broadcasting House
calling us over the air waves from England?

'London calling The Empire! Calling The Empire!
Come in Nigeria.' *I'm coming! I'm coming!*

I shouted at night into the warm winds on deck.
Mama, my dreams have been my fuel for years,

all those British films for sixpence at the movie house.
See London, then die. I was desperate to get here.

When I finally landed in Liverpool it was Heaven,
I had hoped for snow but it was just very cold.

These people run everywhere and wear mufflers.
Older cousin Sam came to greet me at the docks,

just as well because I thought the fast automobiles
would kill me. I asked Sam if many people are killed

by cars. He laughed, 'You will get used to life here.'
The Africans have European wives and sailor's children.

Sam has a house in Princess Park in Toxteth District,
his wife Maureen is Irish and their six-year-old

daughter is Beatrice. I said, 'Why a white wife, Sam?'
He replied, 'When in Rome do as the Romans do.'

Mama, I will write a letter soon, I promise you.

SAM SAYS this country is like fisherman's bait, Mama.
It attracts, you bite, then you are trapped. I told him

I'd be here five years, get my degree and leave.
Tomorrow I head for London. Centre of the Empire!

Sam drinks stout every night complaining that John Bull
only gives him work on the railways, and I've met elders

in the Yoruba club in Croxteth Street who came
in the last century as stowaways and seamen,

fought in two world wars for Britain, but believe
back home is paradise. I argue Nigeria is small time.

Why eat rice and stew when you can taste Yorkshire pud,
meat and two veg? You can buy anything here,

there are so many shops, pubs on every street corner
and houses have all the modern conveniences.

Many people are respectful but some idiots shout
'Oi! Johnny! Sambo! Darkie! Nigger!' at us.

The elders tell us to take no nonsense from them,
so if I am abused I say quietly, 'Just call me Taiwo,'

and boof! I fight them. Even the West Indians say
'Do you people still live in trees in the bush?'

Mama, in this country I am coloured.
Back home I was just me.

MY NICKNAME is Bill now, after William the Conqueror.
I have found that an African name closes doors.

You would not believe the size of London, Mama,
but people live like mice, scurry into their houses

at night and draw the curtains. The streets are quiet
as cemeteries. You think they are dead, but come

morning they unlock their doors, charge back down
the pavement as if life is somewhere else. If I say

'Hello' they are frightened or angry or cross the road.
When we coloureds laugh freely they scowl at us

and on the Underground everyone stares into space.
I need warm clothes because it is so cold and heating

is expensive: the sun avoids this country, Mama.
I found a room in Kilburn for one pound a week,

the family were nice, the wife gave me Sunday dinner
but now I rent a cheaper room in Brixton where many

immigrants live. The landlord is Polish, the wife – Irish
and strict. No phone calls in or out. No visitors.

It is so hard to find a good place to live here
because they do not want us in their houses.

Mama, I have not written you a letter yet but
you must know that I think of you and Kehinde often.

WINTER'S arthritic trees lace evening's broody sky,
miniature waterfalls mid-motion frozen from sloping

roof gutters; window frames display icicles –
January's modern sculptures; bushes drip ephemeral jewellery,

coughing coal fires steam quartered panes like frost.
Chimneys, ordered as sentries, discharge bulbous smoke;

buses crawl through blizzards past snow-filled bomb craters,
faceless back-to-backs, timbers dangling mid-air

like dismembered limbs, winds creaking, no-man's-land.
                                        For men are needed

to replace the fallen dead. In the War like cards
stacked one by one they fell. A clarion call bugled

the colonies, and to a city burnt out from doodlebug
and Luftwaffe, they doffed cap, donned greatcoat,

dreams of prosperity, milk and gold, they were sold.
                                        Now the emperor's disowned sons

congregate in Commonwealth dance halls.
At the Catholic Overseas Club, Victoria, Taiwo,

proud of his zoot suit and loafers, partners the excited,
nubile paleskins who flock in from the snow

for the heat brought in from the tropics.

ELLEN thought British boys danced like ironing-boards.
The students from Strawberry Hill's Jesuit College

sought the pristine convent ladies of Maria Assumpta
at Kensington's balls, tantalised by copious layers

of pink sequinned tulle, boned strapless tops, stoles,
corsage, lace gloves, silk purse and score cards.

Fearful of being lumped with the miserable wallflowers,
Mary with the hare lips and Deirdre with the hairy lip,

Ellen waltzed under the ballroom's cut-crystal chandeliers
with earnest, pallid suitors to bland, suited dance bands

but before the stroke of twelve, Assumpta's flushed
Cinderellas were gliding exquisitely through hushed

lamp-lit streets to curfew and their rooms in the Square.
Sunday mornings in the refectory, Ellen relished tales,

along with tea and buttered toast, of the Overseas Club, Victoria,
brimming with foreign students of the darker variety,

and before long her twitching antennae led her
to the jumping church hall where she jitterbugged

to rock 'n'roll, did the quickstep to swing, while Taiwo,
from his discreet observation post by the door, beamed

at the homely type in polka dot dress, a shy dimpled smile,
and knew she was the girl he would take for a wife.

ELLEN wanted to marry the Heavenly Bridegroom,
imbued from birth in the sanctity of the Catholic Church,

she worshipped Her Lord in daily prayer, did penance
for man's original sin and her inherent wickedness.

She embraced suffering for infinite Love and Happiness
awaited her at the Eternal Bridal Feast in the Sky.

A life of love, duty, self-sacrifice to God and souls
would be embodied in her role as a White Sister,

a teaching missionary enlightening the dark continent.
This Assumpta virgin bought black babies from photographs,

paid for their upkeep, for they who were born in the southern wild
(she read) were bereft of light, though their souls were white,

although white as an angel was the English child.
She adored the choir nuns of the Assumption, well-to-do

women who as postulants gave their wealth to the convent,
striking medieval figures in purple habits, lush as drapes,

topped by a cream wimple, leather belt, rosary, crucifix.
Unlike the lay nuns in plain black and white, consigned

to stir the stewing pot with floor-scrubbed hands.
Ripe for the plucking, Her Purity, small wonder, then

that Ellen's divine lover came in the guise of Taiwo
and in His Vivacious Company her heart was elevated

by cherubim and seraphim who trilled sweetly in her ears
and she was thrilled to be in his Noble Presence.

THE SUPREME test of submission to the Will of God
was the acceptance of pain; life was not to be a joyride,

but during the spring of Nineteen Fifty-two, Ellen,
hitherto shaped in the fashion of clay spun into a pot,

lived with a passion she'd reserved for the hereafter.
With Taiwo umbilically attached she bubbled, unbearably

excited like a five-year-old on Christmas Eve; to him
she revealed the goodies of a country he'd only known

as a stranger peering through snug windows on icy nights.
His tour began with *Seven Brides for Seven Brothers*

in the neon-lit cinema of London's Leicester Square;
boating on the Serpentine's waveless waters filled

Sunday afternoons along with rambles on Hampstead's
wild city heath; trains to Epping Forest – picture postcard

picnics of cheese, pickles, apples, orangeade,
under fairytale ancient trees; cycle rides over London's

evening bridges following the liquid curve of the Thames
from the Tower to the glamorous lights of Chelsea Bridge;

Soho's tempting finger beckoned on busy Friday nights
to Hi-life basement dives replete with émigrés and sailors,

or quiet tea-sipping at Lyons Corner House on the Strand.
Soon, betrothal to The Son was replaced by devotion

to potential husband and dreams of a huge brood
of children so lots of souls could be saved in Heaven.

ELLEN

YOU WILL go to your husband as an uncrushed flower,
I fondly recall Mother Superior's eloquent sermon,

delivered to the sixth form, my last day at school.
I am so proud to know that simile will prevail for me.

It is a summer evening, warm as I imagine Taiwo's land.
I write at my oak desk overlooking Kensington Square;

the scent of honeysuckle travels in through my open window
from the flower-filled gardens where young lovers linger.

I think I have always felt worthless, really, of no account,
yet he makes me feel so important, I am so loved by him.

He phones me every day and I feel cherished.
I cannot believe how my love for Taiwo grows daily.

I love him with every limb, every bone, each beat of my heart,
every thought of my weak brain, every living part of me.

I love him more than life, until I die and go home to God.
I wanted to help Africa but Africa was brought to me.

My friends Mavis, Gwennie and Amy are overjoyed.
We will graduate as teachers, marry our beloveds,

go forth and multiply. My childhood has now been shed
as a caterpillar leaves its chrysalis, only to be recalled

as witty anecdotes to entertain my darling Taiwo
on winter's cosy, married, muffin-toasting nights.

CHAPTER 2

Abbey Wood, London, 1935 –

BABY ELLEN was the cherished, cuddled, coddled,
much-loved child born to Peggy and Leslie Brinkworth.

Pampered with soaps, creams, powders; babyhood
was a perpetual playpen of squeezy, squeaky, squirty,

soft, fluffy and furry things. Nursery rhymes
seduced her to sleep, tinkering bells roused her awake,

oohs, aahs and eyes followed her every movement.
After seven years of a scrimping and saving courtship

to purchase a new house, cash down (£560) *and* furnish it,
the wedded two were overjoyed with their reproduction

ensconced each morning, horizontally gurgling,
to take air in her black bassinet perambulator in the garden.

At No 31 Manton Rd in the new town of Abbey Wood,
Peggy, slight of build, sleight of hand, mind revolving

like a Spinning Jenny, was bent all hours over her noisily
whizzing sewing-machine until her vertebrae stiffened

and the usually punctilious stitches ran into themselves.
When Peggy lifted her screaming infant to becalm her,

she felt no dividing line between their warm bodies,
mother and daughter were seamlessly inseparable –

she knew their paths would be overlocked forever.

PEGGY

I POUR dreams onto Ellen like syrup on treacle tart,
she's growing up a real lady with her bows and ruffles.

Her manners are impeccable, she minds her Ps and Qs,
there are no temper tantrums in public or private

and no playing in the street – she's not common.
A little on the clumsy side, she's given to stubborn moods

but I'll iron that out of her over the next two years.
She's at St Saviour's Primary, then she'll pass the 11 Plus,

get a scholarship to St Joseph's private grammar in Erith,
then university, God willing, and a successful career.

I'm one of life's triers. I don't give up. My home is spotless.
A quick flick with the duster each morning keeps dirt down

then a thorough going-over of a Saturday gets at the invisible.
I detest sloppiness, there's not a thing out of place in No 31.

From the bay window in my living-room I see ninety degrees
of clear sky. In the summer at sunset it's so beautiful –

the purples, reds and golds, all smouldering like a coal fire.
If you work hard your dreams do come true, I'm proof.

The neighbours are a bind, a nosy lot, as soon as I step
outside nets start twitching. But I'm no cause for complaint.

I make sure my windows are as spotless as anybody's.

MY HUSBAND Leslie walks like a subaltern on parade,
stiff as wood and sticks his chest out like a peacock.

German, on his mother's side – the Wilkenings.
As for his father's side: uncouth with no table manners.

Leslie's a Master Dairyman, clippity-clops
his horse and cart at dawn. Likes the silence, he says.

He wears thick glasses so I can't always read his thoughts.
He's sweet but ineffectual. No 'Get-up-and-go,' I tell him.

One of his sisters, Vera, died before he was born.
Always one who dies. Our Edna went at twenty-three,

When I visited the hospital with little Ellen, Winnie
cried because she couldn't cuddle her. Contagious.

We were all screened. It was a terrible time.
I'm closest to Violet, she works in the Gillette factory.

Dora's the youngest, we pay her fees for teachers' training college.
She's being courted now by Jacob: a doctor, a German, a Jew.

You should've seen Ma when she met him. She almost fell
on her knees and kissed his hands like he was the Pope.

A doctor in the family. Well, we're all hoping.

PEGGY invested in the future, the past – a pit to fall down,
but sometimes memory was stronger than the mind

and there she was, sweet Margaret 'Peggy' Robbins,
whose long brown ringlets bounced down to her waist,

whose white cotton petticoats were always starched,
whose button-up boots were always hand-me-downs,

looking up as the strange Zeppelin bird glided overhead,
or the wonderful Corpus Christi procession paraded

before her in Little Italy where they lived, the dazzling
monstrance held up by the priest, golden rays shooting

out from The Host, older Italianate girls from church
wearing white veils and walking ceremoniously behind

a statue of Our Lady on a stretcher, scattering petals.
Or long-dead Gran appeared at No 31, Old Emma Robbins –

an apparition in front of the front parlour's coal fire,
come to pull Peggy back to a childhood where Gran

was a shapeless sack of black in front of the hearth:
black bonnet, rustling skirts, gnarled, brown-spotted

hands knitting blankets. Not talking to anyone – 'living',
muttering in a language only she could understand.

EMMA was delivered into her mamaí's dying arms
in a damp cottage in the frozen wasteland of winter

just as the reign of the Great Hunger was coming
to a close. Its monster jaws had ravaged the island

for four murderous years, masticated the emaciated
bodies of a million poor souls, sucked the flesh

off them and buried their bones in earth blighted
with potatoes rotting with black and green mould.

Britannia, the Protestant Conqueror, who'd long ago
throttled Catholic Hibernia between her two

mammoth hands and stamped it to the ground,
did little to help, inventing scapegoats instead.

Ireland is a human swinery, an abomination,
a black howling Babel of superstitious savages –

like Widow Caitlin, who raised her grandchild Emma
in the iron crook of her arm; who'd lost five daughters

to the Hunger, her husband to Typhus, her only son Lorcan
to the exodus to find work overseas. But oh no not she.

Caitlin swore to the Good Lord that she would raise
at least one grandchild in her beloved homeland

and she made young Emma swear on the Holy Bible
never, ever to abandon Ireland.

'THEY WANT to make us suckle Sasanach words,
to cut out our own sweet Gaelic tongue at the root,'

Caitlin told Emma, gripping the skipping child
in the vice of her hand as they crossed the sun-sprinkled

fields after Sunday's long morning service,
their bare feet sinking into the swill of the rains.

'A curse be upon those that invented laws
to persecute Catholics in this, God's own country.'

In the woods, Emma ran ahead to pick bluebells,
the sun dappled her tattered cream smock,

long black hair a twisted rope down her back.
'How dare they rob us of our right to Home Rule.

That evil bastard Cromwell is to blame.
I'd like to ring his bloody neck,' she called out,

looking around as if he was lurking somewhere.
Emma ran into Caitlin's arms, who cupped her face,

'You've got the face of a man called Turlough,
one of the rebels deported to prison in that faraway

place called Australia in 1798. Remember his name,
Emma, because he was my daidí, and I loved him,

and your great seanathair, and only the Lord
knows how he suffered and died – because I don't.

Oh, but I'd like to cut off the balls of every one
of them Redcoat Sasanach soldiers in town.'

CAITLIN/EMMA

SURE IT'S a peat hovel, but it's our home.
Lorcan's money from London isn't enough.

Uncle Lorcan tried to send for me,
but Mamó shouted 'Over my dead body!'

We eat pheasant and trout to grow her strong.
Old Braden the gamekeeper will never catch me.

Mamó brushes my hair hard every day.
One hundred strokes to keep it shiny.

Rainwater collects in a barrel like noisy drums.
In summer we bathe in the River Camcor.

Mamó sings to me by candlelight.
Outside I see glow worms in the hedgerows.

She's off to that school place for the learning.
Most of Lorcan's money goes on the fees.

I can read and I can write and I can count
and I can be good or I can get a right ear-slapping.

She's on at me to take the donkey track into Birr;
the temptation, now she's older, of soldiers.

I want to see Parson's Castle and the shops,
the square, the fancy houses and all those people.

I'll never let on the awful shame of her mamaí –
how there was no husband to speak of.

These nights I hold Mamó's body.
Her ribcage barely moves. I worry.

How I prayed my country would be liberated
by the time the Good Lord came for me.

EMMA

I AWOKE
cuddling a chilly
bough

Never
been
alone afore

found
in woods
hair like bracken

Mamó
planted back
in soil

I would not
dishonour her
by leaving Éire

begging – for me?
workhouse – for me?
service – for me?

door to door
he
knocks

I ran
into the woods
and rained

like a squirrel
I
forage

Uncle Lorcan
arrived
a stranger

dirt shovelled
on grey face I
choked

you're as stubborn
as my mother
he said

I fly
in the grip
of his hand

my bare feet
his black boots
castle gravel, crunch

CHAPTER 3

Parson's Castle, Birr, Ireland

CHINTZ, carpets, mahogany, marquetry,
porcelain, damask, bronzes, curtains, chinoiserie,

brass fittings, flagstone floors, ormolu mounts,
rosewood, black-lacquer, Persian rugs,

a sofa veneered with rosewood, plinths inlaid
with stylised arabesques with coil-sprung seats

for comfort; a walnut commode; a red marble-topped
table on a carved frieze above a central column

with spiral fluting surrounded by sphinxes;
a floor-length mirror with a carved softwood frame;

enormous stained-glass windows; ten bed chambers,
a drawing-room, breakfast room, dining-room,

games room, smoking room, garden room, terrace
room, ballroom, library, a medieval tower, ice house,

kitchen garden, lake, box hedges, fernery, fountain,
waterfall, trout pond, deer park, gazebos,

a beech-lined drive, and, in the steaming, belching
bowels of the castle, the cavernous kitchen

where Emma spends her every waking moment,
and the moist cellar next door, where she sleeps.

EMMA

I'M THE SCULLERY MAID, the skivvy, the flunky
in Mr Mallory's empire – the kitchen.

Up before dawn to scrape ash from the range,
black-lead it, light it, then keep it going all day.

Then it's breakfast for Lord Harrington, his wife
and their two 'flawless beauties' my age, so I'm told.

Kidneys, kedgeree, tongue, ham, cold game pie,
woodcock, bacon, boiled, fried or poached eggs,

mushrooms straight from the dark house, toast –
most of which they waste anyway. (More for me.)

When I arrived years ago the sight of all that food
made me quite sick. (Gout and good riddance to them.)

For dinner it's soup, fish dish, three meat dishes,
a savoury and a dessert all served *à la Russe*

from the sideboard by footmen who are *obsequious*
to their superiors and *condescending* to the likes of me.

I believe in words. I read them, remember them,
load them into my mouth – and fire.

ONLY WAY to escape is through marriage.
The local fellows? *Philanderers! Braggadocios!*

I tell them to 'go fuck' themselves too.
Mamó would be so proud of me.

Mr Mallory used to brush against my breasts
until one day I said, 'Leave off my *appendages*, Sir'

in front of Mrs Mallory, the housekeeper, wife.
(Poor man, fancy waking up next to a bulldog?)

Had me sieving rhubarb consommé for hours after that.
Not seen Uncle Lorcan since he brought me here.

He writes at Christmas but Mr Kempster the butler
opens our letters in the pantry, *sullying* them.

Uncle Lorcan says there's a home for me in London.
He's old now, even his children have children,

but Mamó would rise from the dead,
wispy hair stuck about her like a dusty spider's web,

and walk through these thick castle walls, howling.
I might finish at midnight, or dawn, if there's a ball,

I can hear the waltzes and unstoppable merriment.
Before sleep I sit up reading by candlelight.

Pride and Prejudice is my favourite. Enya is a ladies
maid upstairs. She *appropriates* books for me.

I'VE ALREADY won some green ribbons at the staff fair
in the three-legged race with Enya. (How exciting.)

Seen the performing horses and the mind-reading dog.
I've swung my hips brazenly inside a hoola-hoop,

tried croquet, and I'm in the queue to climb the greasy pole
for a slice of plum pie (Isn't His Lordship *munificent?*)

when I see my future husband's head immersed in a bowl
before coming up with a green apple in his mouth.

Spluttering, he shakes water from his hair like a horse,
and I can see he is all manliness and sparkling

charisma and wavy brown hair and shiny brass buttons
and God only knows why but I run over, pluck

the apple from between his clean, *symmetrical* teeth
and shriek as he chases me behind the box hedges

whereupon we fall to the ground, panting.
He slips his hand in mine and I break a sweat.

His fingers are calloused, muscular and warm –
yet I can feel music pass through them.

THE MIRACLE of his wet tongue in combat with mine.
His moustache, scratchy as sand used to scour pans.

Big brass buttons pressing into my breastbone.
I could see bits of myself melting in them.

Private Henry Robbins was a handsome man,
his hardness made me feel so soft and spongy.

My skirts and drawers spread about me like petals.
My bones were blazing coals; my blood molten.

His fingers parted my plaits then *curlicued* my hair.
The night's cool breath caressed my nakedness.

My butterfly breasts were touched for the first time.
His skin peeled off, wrapped around mine.

My brain had grown wings and flown to the moon.
No one had ever told me – the *exquisite* pleasure.

How could something so delicious ever be wrong?
The speed at which he unbuckled without fumbling.

He slid into me and when I opened my eyes to scream
without sound, there standing high above us,

erect as the tall statue of Oliver Cromwell in town,
was Mamó, monstrous against the royal-blue sky.

High-necked, arms crossed, she shook her head,
and worked her lips: 'Fil-thee. Turn-coat. Whooo-re.'

HE WAS so dashing marching in the parades,
straight-backed, shiny-booted, blowing his bugle

beautifully, winking at me when he passed,
making my cheeks flush and the other girls jealous.

And when he was off quelling another Fenian uprising,
I prayed Mamó would forgive me.

And when the bump that became Mary Jane showed,
thanks be to God he married me, and quickly.

Mr Mallory (of all people) had to give me away
when Uncle Lorcan wrote saying he wasn't going

to dance with the Devil on his mother's grave.
He kept to his own in London. *It's come to this.*

You might be my niece, Emma, but it's goodbye.
My English soldier loved his 'little Irish lass' to bits,

but forbade the speaking of Gaelic in our house.
'Can't have my two girls plotting against me.'

Mary Jane was a water-babby, trying to catch fish
in the river, or splashing about when it rained.

But the summer her bones grew longer than mine,
the local harvest failed and I committed my second

cardinal sin: we set sail for England.

CHAPTER 4

Seven Dials, London, 1880 –

THE SWEATY armpit of London: the seven septic
streets of sore-raddled Seven Dials welcomed

the Robbins' family into its flea-infested embrace:
a windowless dungeon in a collapsing tenement

in a yard without water or sunlight at the end
of an alley running slimy with effluence.

This was where the newly-arrived washed up –
green-eyed, open-mouthed, desperate, forced

to cohabit with robbers, ruffians, rouged harlots,
to endure the torture of endlessly clattering carts,

grating knife-grinders, beggars, dog-breakers,
parrot-sellers, herring-hawkers, metal-workers,

of brawling drunks and bawling women in labour.
Oh, how they suffocated in summer's grease-slathered

mugginess, its toothless, foul-mouthed breath,
particles of coal dust coating once-healthy lungs.

> Never again the evensong of nightingales in the woods,
> Never again the percussive patter of rain on the Camcor.
> Never again the crisp, clean oxygen of home – Ireland.

EMMA

EVERYTHING'S all right
until I open my pretty Irish mouth
and see the words *Bog-trotter* lumber
like the Great White Ape they think I am across
the cavities they call brains.

Mary Jane is full of cheek.
The harlots downstairs call her their 'half-breed'.
Any time she wants a job...

Swallowed my pride like a lump of coal.
Called upon Uncle Lorcan.
Calmel Buildings, Marylebone.

Woollen shawl hugged against trembling cold,
blue-crusted feet quite bare, I was so thin
my cheekbones showed
like sharp stones.

Old, bowed, his long grey hair flowed:
Now you know.
Go back to your redcoat soldier, Traitor.
I told you a long, long time ago,
you have been disowned.

HENRY

'HENRY Robbins of Brackley, Northamptonshire,
formerly of the 3rd Leinster Brigade, stationed

at Crinkle Barracks, Ireland,' I say, seeking work
door-to-door in this dog-eat-dog hellhole.

Took to scavenging on rubbish heaps to save us
from starving, while Emma took Mary Jane to comb

the riverbank for things to salvage and sell.
Got a better job, eventually, picking up horse dung,

while the girls got a penny a peck shelling peas
in Covent Garden. Heck, we were on the up and up.

Look, the Army never prepared me for civilian life.
I went in at fifteen and just obeyed orders.

Truth is, I left my dignity behind in Ireland,
working head of my family, coming home Saturdays

with a hare or rabbit dangling from my belt.
Most nights I'm to be found at Baxters Beer House,

playing blackjack for a pint or two (or three), trying
to escape the malice in the wife's smile, the gunpowder

fired from the barrel of her mouth: *Gobshite!*
And, when I take what's mine at night: *Dee-bawched!*

TWENTY of us last time in the Black Maria.
Only three women, the prettiest were jumped.

Kind of behaviour I'd last seen in the army
when we stormed whole villages in the Uprisings.

If you object, your card is marked. So you don't.
I'm an embarrassment to my withering little missus,

her words minced with arsenic: *Addlebrained cretin!*
Only time I get photographed is in Newgate.

'Dashing'? – not passed the wife's lips for years.
Very fetching – is my hardened convict look.

Mary Jane writes letters, silly when I can't read.
Only time I have a bath is inside. The water's

a muddy brown because they don't change it.
Won't mention the screw's personal 'inspections'.

Scramble for old boots on arrival, humiliation
of a scarlet shirt and trousers, shaved, a new name,

(No 121), dining on the delights of bread and gruel.
If I get into a fight, it's the treadmill grinding cereals

for months. Must learn to bite my lip,
even when they do ask after my 'Bog-Trotter' wife.

MARY JANE

ONE HUNDRED children in this classroom and still
Miss Carter has to have a go at 'Mary Jane!'

Then she's taking the birch out of its jar of water
so's it's soft enough to slide across my bare legs.

If I was a lad I'd wallop her back. Some do.
The windows are so high we can't see out,

and if I have to write down another dictation
on a slate about sunflowers and snails I'll run

outside and throw myself under an omnibus.
What use is Reading, wRiting and aRithmetic

when Ma can do two of those and has nothing?
Soon as I'm twelve I'm leaving school so's

she don't have to work so hard for a pauper's pittance,
what with silly old Da banged up again in Newgate.

Do Right and Fear Not is our school motto.
Punctuality. Industry. Obedience. Regularity.

Oh yes, I'm that all right, every morning after tea
and bread dripping, sliding down the banisters

to the toilet outside 5 Elm Court, St Pancras.

EMMA

MY HANDS are crab's claws.
Knuckles just won't straighten.

Too blind to thread a needle.
Vertebrae's like a crooked finger.

Knit blankets from old wool.
A Bermondsey trader collects.

The world outside is dangerous:
carriages and savages.

I want to go home.
Should never have wed an Englishman.

Seduced by brass buttons and shiny boots.
He's got no *gumption.*

Cost me my ticket to the Pearly Gates.
I'll burn in Hell.

HENRY

NO PLEASING the narky wife.
Hard to imagine what I saw in her.

Wrinkled: face, neck, hands.
Don't see the rest, thank God.

Lasses used to scrap over me.
Not been inside for eight years.

Thanks? She don't speak to me.
Odd jobs. Labouring. Not well.

Liver disease. Turning yellow.
Mary Jane makes dresses.

She brings home the bacon.
The old bat couldn't give me a son.

Come to think of it –
were the wife what drove me to drink.

MARY JANE

SEBASTIAN Aloysius Burt.
Glassblower – a proper trade.

His mother Bertha shares our lodgings.
That's how we met.

Ma had a word, 'He's not Irish…'
'Neither is your husband,' I retorted.

Did she want me to die a spinster?
Want my own little ones.

Got dribbling parents instead.
Seb's stocky, teetotal, sensible.

His dad died fighting the Zulus.
Single-handedly, he makes it sound.

Walks me up Oxford Street
after morning Mass on Sundays.

Told him I've plans to go to Heaven.
One of those big houses up at the Angel.

CHAPTER 5

MARY JANE and Sebastian got hitched in Holborn
the year the red line of the Tuppenny Tube

was added to London's subterranean railway,
and the Labour Party was launched for the working man,

and influenza killed thousands and the Great British Public
was asked to cough up for the second Boer War,

and pleasure steamers ploughed the Thames like Nile barges,
and the newlyweds honeymooned downriver to Kew

to see the banana palms and bamboos from the colonies
and the famous Pagoda and Amazonian Water Lily,

then back to the Embankment at twilight to hail
a penny-a-mile Hansom Cab to the Grand Café Royal

on Regent's Street where pearl-throated ladies
swished inside wearing chiffon and lace, satin and crepe,

while they stood opposite, under the haze of a street lamp,
Mary Jane's light green dress brushing the ground,

Sebastian, a foot shorter, in a black suit and trilby,
fingers lovingly entwined, on this – the most glamorous,

most hopeful, most à la carte day of their lives.

MARY JANE

THE PICTURE OF DORIAN GRAY by Oscar Wilde.
I read it to Ma most nights, now she's gone blind.

Her venomous tongue still darts out like a snake's
even though Da passed on a few years since.

She won't accept her Englishman son-in-law.
Same one who buys her books at W. & G. Foyle

on Charing Cross Road, though he can ill afford it.
Some shops are not for the likes of us:

Marshall & Snelgroves, John Lewis, Selfridges.
They turf you out. We're market people:

Billingsate, Spitalfields, Berwick St. We hover outside
then Seb smooths down the front of the linen

suit I made at Madame Percherons – narrow trousers,
natty boater and struts inside, me all red-faced behind.

He strides up to the counter with his mighty little legs,
and adopts the most preposterous well-to-do accent,

ignoring the clerk's smirk as he shoos us to an aisle
where I find the right book. (Seb can't read.)

> We sneak out the side door – like we're thieves.
> We sneak out the side door – and breathe.

MARY JANE stitched food into her children's mouths,
clothes onto their bodies. Peggy, the eldest, helped out.

Sebastian returned home from inhaling glass late,
chest rattling as he caught his breath on the landing.

In two rented rooms at No 20 Upper Street
eight children crawled like bugs over furniture

bought on the cheap from Arkwrights second-hand,
and Mary Jane bemoaned a toilet thirty flaming

stairs down, balancing infants and chamber pots
on her hips, a kitchen that wasn't her own

and a mother who sat knitting and cursing her daughter
until the undertaker's stretcher came for her.

Mary Jane blamed Sebastian for not being rich.
Should be living in a great house up at Highgate.

Nine bedrooms. Bathrooms. Drawing rooms. Nursery.
Nannies. Maids. Library. Conservatory. Cook.

High tea. Pearls. Parties. Rose garden. Rockery. Lawn.
Morning constitutional on Hampstead Heath.

(Daughters presented at court, while I'm at it.)

THE PAST framed itself into a child-crowded doorway,
Peggy's seven siblings looked up at her through the years,

There she was, fourteen years in her, the obedient eldest,
whitening her knuckles against a washboard with soap,

cleaning windows with scrunched-up newspaper and vinegar,
plaiting newspaper to start coal fires, scraping the grate,

fetching the coal from the hole four floors down
in the basement, bathing the smallest in a tin tub

of hand-me-down, tepid water, checking
for lice, dirt behind ears, under fingernails, toenails,

boiling soiled nappies and towels on the stove, peeling
innumerable spuds for stew, the peelings for compost

to be dug into the vegetable patch in spring's softer soil.
Between chores Peggy hemmed herself out of adolescence,

apprenticed to her mother's pernickety tuition, making
velvet evening gowns, elaborate lacy wedding dresses.

She imagined balls and finery, envied the porcelain dolls'
hands of the la-di-dahs who came for fittings, rejected

her station in life; aspired to a husband, a child, a home
of her own, and entry to the middle classes.

PEGGY

'THE SKY'S a bowl of dirty washing-up water.
I have to crane my neck forty-five degrees and squint

up past grimy buildings to see some tainted blue.
I want to see a lovely bird-span of sky where I live.'

Peggy cut a pattern out of newspaper with large scissors,
hands moving steadily across the wooden floor,

voice light with a whispery, breathless wistfulness.
'Everything I do keeps my head down, fixed on work

but when Leslie and I marry we'll share a sky together.'
Mary Jane responded to her eldest's fancies, a grim smile

as she threaded cotton through a miniscule hole,
her voice once lyrical as a trickling stream, hardened

by stunted desires, nasalised by city concrete.
'You'll do better than I did, then, and you could do worse.

He's of business stock, not the wondering type, reliable,
and he can probably take a good tongue-lashing.

A husband who can be jollied along is best.'
'One thing's for sure, Ma, I won't end up in pokey rooms

sharing your neighbour's washing line and smelly toilet.'
'You're a cheeky wretch, aren't you. Love's a ladder, Peggy.

He's suitable, first and foremost. Just work hard
so's your children enter the professions or marry

into them. I don't want any grandchildren of mine
rolling about in the gutter.'

CHAPTER 6

Abbey Wood, London, 1939 –

PEGGY

THE SIRENS sounded, an eerie deafening wail,
and we prepared for war. We got blue ration cards

and gas masks which made us look like deep sea-horses.
Blackouts, sandbags and shelters became daily words

but the planes didn't come, we called it the Phoney War.
Ellen was upset, 'Why didn't we have the war today, Mummy?'

she moaned as if war was a present from Father Christmas.
A week later we took her to Liverpool Street Station

to be evacuated with Dora and her pupils to the country.
Leslie and I couldn't look at each other in case

our pain shot out like a burst water pipe. It wouldn't do.
I feared we'd become an early childhood memory to Ellen,

like a forgotten doll she'd fondly recall as an adult.
I told her to be good, tidy and that we both loved her

even more than jelly, jam sponge, mince pies *and* toffee.
Her grey eyes looked so lovely when I kissed her little nose.

Please. Please. I prayed, *Keep my dearest safe and happy.*
Outside the station, London was a city of swarming bees,

children were being swept, carried and dragged inside.
I told Leslie to pray to God that we would all survive.

We caught the train home and waited for the bombs.

I WAS in the kitchen slicing ham for afternoon tea
when the Blitz finally hit us in early September.

I dashed down to our Anderson shelter in the garden,
that ugly monstrosity of corrugated iron slap bang

in the corner where my rhododendrons used to grow.
Leslie and I sat impatiently, waiting for the all-clear,

but for the first time in a year it never came. Oh Lordy!
I prayed so hard I was a muttering twit clasping

my rosary for the twelve hours we spent in that dankness.
Thunderous explosions outside made Guy Fawkes Night

sound like the Mad Hatter's Tea Party, and I felt as if
my bones were cracking into pieces like broken crockery.

When the all-clear went I dreaded that No 31 would be
a pile of bricks, torn wallpaper, bed springs and smoke.

That's how it went on for the fifty-six nights following.
I felt buried alive like an Egyptian slave in a tomb.

Come morning I'd air our bedding in front of the fire,
and more steam would pour out than in a Chinese laundry.

It was like that off and on for nine months and by then
over twenty thousand of us had gone under.

DEW shivers on wild grass blades – tremulous tears.
The fields are crying as they climb upwards

in boundaries of hedges away from the bumpy road
ambling downwards, a thin veneer of rain like a still stream.

Mist blurs this rural vista, the grey of a painter's brush
sweeps over trees clustered tightly into woods,

the tiny thatched village of Necton, sloping at the forked
bend by the silent church, where a mud-ridged lane

wends up to Necton Hall, obscured by clouds, its fairy
tale cupolas, turrets, gables ornate as a crown.

Morning's lukewarm sun peers over low-lying hills
onto the octagonal cottage on the estate – the folly.

Its pagoda chimneys, stable door and church windows
are home to Auntie Dora and Ellen, their war-time billet,

the child now playing hopscotch on the flagstone floor.
When the sun finally bears down to unfurl flowers,

Ellen is scooting outside after breakfast, cycling the vast
acres of empty playground with her new friend Gerard,

the gamekeeper's curly, red-haired son with freckles.
Their giggles bubble behind hills as they roll down

a long green slope stopping just short of the muddy lane.
From the manicured gardens of No 31 to the echoing hills

of Necton, Ellen grew into her wildness without hiccups.

REDCURRANT, blackcurrant, blackberries, gooseberries
grow everywhere to be gorged by the voracious two

between hide-and-seek in the woods and on-the-hop pees
behind bushes. Gerard crowned the straggly-haired Ellen

the Buttercup Princess with a garland of flowers
before racing her to the walls of the Hall where injured

soldiers recuperated in the absence of the owner
who'd 'gorn orf' to the Bahamas for the duration.

When cold sunk the countryside several feet in snow
and building snowmen was boring, Gerard battered

Ellen's toys on the floor, just like a soldier, he said, sneering
at her cry-baby tears over beheaded dolls and gutted teddies.

'You bully, you!' she screeched before storming
off to Auntie Dora, whom she knew adored her.

Term time Dora taught evacuees in the village school,
holidays she picked fruit, made jam, trifles, soups

while the laughing pair threw mud pies at each other,
squelched their feet in mud, their hair clotted dollops

until Dora threw pails of water on their pale squirming
bodies then scrubbed them down until their skins flushed.

Night-time she snuggled Ellen to bed and told her to pray
for her parents, orphans and the war's sorry suffering.

VISITORS glide through the folly like woodland fairies,
their visits gilded treats, bringers of goodies, transient.

Wintertime, Jacob brought a toboggan made in Hamburg,
shipped over when he fled the Nazis in the Thirties.

Like a reindeer he heaved the great 'Alaskan sleigh'
over frozen ponds to the squeals of his delighted passengers.

The quick-click heels of Peggy were heard some weekends
while she 'set the kitchen to rights', she said, tut-tutted

the angles of Ellen's hair into two tidy plaits, slipped
a floral dress over shorts, bemoaned the new-found

exuberance in her usually taciturn child, but let it go –
all creases would be starched out post-war. Her heels

ground into gravel as she briskly waved herself away.
Arms brimming with toys, Auntie Violet's laughter

preceded her fur-draped self. Lounging on the sofa,
regaling wide-eyed Ellen with tales of the war's horrors,

lips dangling a cigarette, whisky kissing her mouth.
She slurred her tottery cheery-byes to a tittering niece

for whom war was homemade lemonade on a daisy-strewn,
sun-soaked field of a shimmering summer's afternoon.

ELLEN

DEAR MUMMY and daddy, thank you for the choklate
very much i had my tooth out last week the fairees
put a sixpence under my pilow. I play very happily with Gerard
we go to school all day. how i like it. we have a teeny weeny
kitten he is blak so auntie dora says we call him lucky.
i love to you from your ellen x.

Dear mummy and daddy. I have a cof and auntie dora
has a cof too so we stay at home. a bomb droppt near us
but we were not hurt. I played on a hay stak with Gerard
but next time it had barbed wire round it and the ladder
was taking away. I cried in bed on monday for you.

Dear Mummy and daddy. Thankyou for your letter.
I read it by myself and I liked it. We had a good bit of snow here.
We have been sliding on a pond. Are you coming
at christmas with lots of surprises for me? I raced home
yesterday but the door was locked so I got in threw a
window and started to lay the tea. I am very happy.
I wrote this in a hurry. Love and kisses your Ellen. x

Dear Mummy and Daddy, I am sorry you have a cold.
We had another lot of snow. Auntie Dora is cleaning the
sitting room this morning. Lucky keeps jumping
on my lap. I like my new cardigan. I am very interesting in it.
Gerard told me my fortune. He said I will polish
his school shoes tonight. Love from your Ellen.x

DEAR GERARD,

London is full of broken buildings.
I miss the hazel woods where we picked bluebells,
Lucky, whom I love so much, and I miss racing you
across the fields like a horse and I even miss your
bullying of me. I miss the snowmen which I built and which
you punched in the face and I miss the rabbits.
When I came home I cried every day for a long time.
Mummy said I was ungrateful because she had been
through hell in the war and I was six years away and she
worried very much and now all I do is cry. She said
some children do not have a mummy and daddy at all.
Mummy said the countryside has made me primitive
like a native swinging through the trees in the jungle, she says
she must tame me the way cowboys do horses in films.
She says I walk like a boy, I am as clumsy as an elephant,
I do not plump my pillows properly and my tummy is too big.
I must not jiggle my feet when I sit and I must
take my elbows off the table when I eat. Mummy says
I must study hard but when I read a story book she says
I am being lazy sitting around doing nothing and I will
end up in a factory if I do not do what she says.
I pray each night that I make her happy and not angry with me.
Love and kisses from your Buttercup Princess. x

DEAR GERARD,

I am now at St Joseph's Convent!
A scholarship girl. Mummy is really pleased with me.
Our school motto is *Death Before Dishonour*. I am not
sure what it means but there was a twelve-year-old girl
called Maria Goretti who died on a hilltop rather
than lose her honour. We said Mass for her at school.
I am so smart in my uniform. My best friends is Maureen
alias Piggy. Her father is a lawyer so Mummy says
she is a good friend to have.
Love from your Buttercup Princess who is now grown up. x

Dear Gerard,

It was such a lovely surprise to get your letter.
Well, I passed my Highers, with God's help, and I am soon
off to Maria Assumpta Teacher's Training College
in *Kensington* in the centre of London.
Sad news to tell. Reverend Mother St Hilda passed away
this term. It was she who inspired me to devote my life
to the service of God. (I told Mummy and she was livid!)
She lay in our chapel, Ker Ana, surrounded by white lilies,
while we filed past in tears. She looked like a waxwork.
It was so sad.
Fondest love from Ellen of olden times. x

CHAPTER 7

THE YEAR Lizbet is crowned, Everest conquered
and Ellen is courted with flowers from Taiwo each week,

who awaits her presence in a stained-glass vestibule
under the slitted-eyes of shadowy nuns who suspect all

suitors are womanisers out to mattress their charges.
In his threadbare bedsit in Atlantic Road, Brixton,

Taiwo plays seducer with his brand new radiogram,
queues of Bing Crosby, Dean Martin and Nat King Cole

ballads glide smoothly down to his suggestive strokes.
But Ellen giggles sex out the window like a rotten apple

for its purpose is solely for babies within marriage,
and Taiwo retracts his slim-fingered attempts to slide

over butter-coloured flesh to unleash rising breasts
caged in a bullet-shaped brassière and succumbs

to the hollow delights of Hollywood kisses instead.
One long night cycle ride from Kensington to Brixton,

Taiwo's mind backpedals to his mother at the docks,
he'd ignored her cry for years: *Taiwo...Taiwo...Taiwo...*

It queased his stomach, nightmared his dreams, jumped
into his thoughts when off-guard throwing him off-centre.

Now was the time to write that letter home..

ZENOBIA

MY DEAR BOY, praise the almighty that you are safe.
How could I have produced such a heartless boy, eh?
It took so long to write a little letter to your mother?
I, who carried you for nine months, suckled and raised you?
My boy, you must *never* forget where you came from.
The news I bring you should be relayed face to face
but as my boy is so far away, pen and paper must suffice.
The scream which sliced through a rainy season night
is ever imprinted on the memories of those who heard it.
It carried no hope, no future, no redemption.
It was your twin, Kehinde, in labour, and by the time
I reached her, she and the child within had lost the battle.
My son, I wailed myself into oblivion for weeks.
But when she began to visit me I put food on her plate.
She tells me it was the juju of your father's women,
to draw my strength so that I could no longer visit them
to claim the land and houses he left me in his will.
I pray the Lord will show them mercy on Judgement Day.
So! You choose an England-lady to woo? Eh! Eh!
Son, there are plenty nice Nigerian girls here.
Come home soon to look after your poor mama.

TAIWO

I BURN UP all night. I burn up   Kehinde   dead
    dead   dead
My sheets are heavy with sweat   dead   Kehinde
    dead   dead

I drown in the water that birthed me   Kehinde   dead

No words. I have no words   dead   Kehinde
My tongue, swollen   dead   dead
Ox tongue stuffed in mouth   Kehinde   dead
    dead   dead
Kehinde why you leave me?   dead   Kehinde
    dead   dead

Mama! Let me crawl back!   Kehinde   dead
Back into your womb, Mama   dead   dead
Undo me. Rock me unborn.   dead   Kehinde
Back to water, back to water   dead   dead

TEARS are for sissies, women and Nancy-boys.
Pain is shit to be flushed down the toilet.

I have taken my heart out, dug a grave for it
and said good riddance. I never want to see it again,

Man was put on this earth to suffer, but not me.
I will make a success of my life and one day

go visit Mama with a suitcase full of green notes.
Ah, life can be good when put into perspective.

Taiwo did not paint his childhood landscape for Ellen,
did not orate the sequence of births and deaths, her mind
should be kept blank, he decided, she need not know.

She is the only person in this country who cares for me.
She is my sonnet, my England-lady, my woman.

When Taiwo withdraws, I am drawn closer to him.
I wonder what thoughts fill his mind? He is so secretive.
Next weekend I'm going to tell Mummy about him.
It's time they met. I wonder what she will say?

'OH! He's not too dark, is he?' Peggy grimaced.
'Pass the butter, dear, and don't slouch. Goodness

knows I've told you enough times. You'll end up
like the hunchback of Notre Dame. Where did

this Tiyowoyo spring from then? What did you
go *there* for? What's wrong with the Strawberry Hill boys

or nice Stephen Brown from church? Of course,
John McBride is ideal but he's off to seminary soon.

Such a waste. At least you've put this nun nonsense
on the scrap heap. A nun indeed. So where does

Tooyamiya hail from? All right, Tie-wo. Bill?
Well, that's better. A native from a colony? Good Lord,

so he *is* dark. Have you no sense of morals?
Look, Ellen, I'm not one to interfere in your affairs

but you must discontinue this liaison immediately.
Do you understand? Good grief, whatever next.

Now, I've baked you a Madeira to take back to college
and I'll run off a summer dress for you this weekend.

I got the pattern out of *Woman's Weekly* on Thursday.
You'll need a fitting though, I've noticed a pudding

bulge appearing. I don't know where you get it from,
must be your father's side. Now off you pop while

I do the dishes. I don't want you under my feet.'

A WORKMAN'S drill reverberates in Ellen's head
as the smoking train growls out of Plumstead Station

rotating laboriously to Charing's burning cross,
her mind a morass of spinning images; her mother's tongue

chiding, lengthening, cracking like a whip into air;
a man pinned up on a crucifix, dying so she could

be saved, crosses, head over heels, plummeting;
African primitives in chorus, cherubic white-starched

children singing hallelujahs to the rhythm of pounding
goatskin drums; ten commandments... *Do Unto Others...*

... *Love Thy Neighbour...* all torn pages floating
one by one into the abyss. Her congealed brain leads

her to the chapel at Maria Assumpta where she kneels,
soft knees squashed on hard leather cushions,

elbows on a dark varnished pew, and her eyes flame
in prayer, reflected in the dancing candles before her,

and from their inner light the Lord's voice answers,
baptismal water fills her head, a clear stream runs through

tinkling *Love Conquers All* and Ellen feels pure once more,
her resolve is born, escorts her uplifted down the aisle

like a groom and out the wooden doors into orange light.

HOPE RISES with the sun over London's spring streets:
mews, lanes, groves, courts, hills and avenues

spawn lavender blossoms, bunched into wedding
posies till a stray breeze floats them singly down

to pattern grey stone slabs awhile. Daffodils sneak up
out of winter, thorned bushes bud the new season

and natives shed dark woollen protectors for light
cotton reflectors; drills jaunt across town, flowers

splayed on gathered frocks have buckle-sucked waists.
a freckled décolletage is offset by imitation pearls

and dried and dyed cows are slipped over arched feet.
Ellen wears cashmere love like a canary-yellow cardigan,

carries hankies in her handbag on weekend trips to No 31,
where Peggy's measured enquiry re the unsuitable beau

is charged with the fear that he has not been expurgated.
Ellen stutters back that he is fine, indeed *they* are fine,

then her breath truncates in her windpipe while Peggy
frenzies a tornado of words over the table and Ellen,

paralysed in the eye of the storm, exhales fear
through a silent sigh and prays for her mother's approval.

TWO VEILED alabaster Madonnas reside as mantelpiece
sentinels on resolute marble, averting pupil-less eyes

from the scene being drawn out by Peggy.
'Ellen, you'll not marry him!' / 'But I love him, Mummy.'

'You must love me more!' Silence hung with the green
velvet curtains, the Victorian grandmother clock

clanged eight hours, the voluptuous sofa prepared, again,
to comfort a tearful Ellen into cushioned arms. Peggy

marched the loomed floor, her stride considered the matter
over, but Ellen's tiny voice hummed the warm furnishings,

'I love him, Mummy, and I want to marry him, that's all.'
Peggy spun round, her voice sliced the air like a scythe,

'*That's* all. *That's* all. After all I've done for you.
Do you think I'm going to let you ruin your life

by marrying a…darkie, a…nigger-man? You *silly* girl.
I have sacrificed my *whole life* for you. How cruel!

How could you do this to me, your *own mother*!'
Peggy gulped a scream down, balled fist to open mouth,

a Greek tragi-mask, then fled the room, stomped upstairs,
slammed her bedroom door, and bawled the house down.

GOSSIPING locals are incensed. A nigger! A darkie!
is whispered over hedges, over counters, at Mass.

An African, cannibal, savage, monkey, heathen,
a thing from outer space. Goodness Gracious No.

Tongues slather, heads gyrate, fingers shake.
His colour will come off on the sheets, p'raps she can

scrub him white, they have tails, you know,
live in mud huts, swing from trees, were idol-worshippers

till we civilised them. For the love of God, whatever
has possessed the girl? Has she no sense of shame, no modesty?

A dark one, they mutter. Dark! Dark! Dark!
No good will come of this, you mark my words.

It's scandalous, it is. Bring the girl to her senses.
Think of the poor children, half-breeds, mongrels.

It's not right bringing them into the world, it isn't.
Oh yes, there she goes, out to meet him. Quick, turn off

the light so she can't see us. Brazen hussy!
Slut! Look at her, trotting along without a care,

who does she think she is, Lady Bleedin' Docker?
For the love of God someone help her see the light.

SKY RIPS it sagging grey hymen with a fingernail,
tanks thunder over Plumstead Common towards No 31.

War is declared by Peggy, self-appointed Chief-of-Staff,
who summons her loyal officers to Army H.Q., briefs

them on her offspring's ignoble insurrection, then
debates how to curtail then corral the wayward Ellen.

Violet flicks ash with contempt for the selfish young.
Dora berates herself for sowing wildness into the girl.

Jacob runs olive fingers through knowing black curls,
and Leslie, reluctant right hand to Napoleon, is more

concerned with the mould in his John Playered throat.
Sky drips onto the tidy rippled roofs of Manton Rd,

aproned wives scurry into gardens to unpeg gymnastic
washing, Peggy trembles thin beige liquid from the trunk

of pregnant china just as God's tears orchestrate
percussive music outside, and two transparent globules

expand out of Peggy's eyes, creep unassailed down
drawn, twitching cheeks while her attentive audience

await her command – the edict? 'The concerted effort
of all those gathered here today will stop, at all costs,

this unspeakable union. So let it be written!'
Then she blows her nose.

A RAINBOW flashes the exhausted sky,
framing low, gleaming buildings and refreshed trees.

The stockinged legs and baggy turn-ups of lovers
cycle joyfully in tandem across the common's mulch

and on down the hill to the pristine terraced houses
where Taiwo deposits his beaming fiancée safely home.

Peggy, hearing foreign rumbles at her gate, flings open
the door, hisses him to go away before the neighbours

see him, shoos him off. Taiwo wheels his pushbike
off the pavement and pedals away, shoulders hunched,

and Ellen feels fury struggle up her windpipe but, unused
to its disturbing sensation, coughs it back down, sees

the despair in her mother's half-open mouth, dashes
past her inside. The sapped sun drops to the east

over Woolwich, its farewell a lingering light as Taiwo
makes his exodus. *How man must suffer*, he sighs.

She judges me but she does not know me.
Oh Mama, these people hate me.

PEGGY'S duck pillows become ponds when Ellen visits,
her night-time sobs are an overflowing bath, journey

from the master bedroom to her daughter's own, seep
steadily under the door like an army's advancing front line,

then crawl up her blanket to claim her. Ellen knows
the ritual: first her mother derides Taiwo's existence,

a volley of machine gun invective ensues, finally,
deflating, she becomes a sodden, spineless

vessel brimming with tears, pleas and cajoling;
her pain – a hive of frightened bees at Ellen's heart.

Faith is the spinal chord which keeps the girl sane.
Were they not all God's children? How very silly!

Why such fuss because of colour? She barely noticed it.
Other times the hoo-haa she caused exhilarated her

for she, who had never put a foot wrong in her life ,
was finally, unequivocally, shamelessly Being Naughty.

A solution to the problem popped into her head as she
Macleaned her teeth one histrionic morning. Her mother

should meet Taiwo, see how nice he was. After all,
she'd never even met a coloured person, but Peggy beat

her to it: 'Bring him to tea!' she shouted upstairs.

'AND HOW MANY wives do you have, Bill?'
A pyramid of trimmed and quartered sandwiches

separated Peggy's high-collar from Taiwo's blue-tied
Adam's apple. Cheddar cheese lay guillotined

on a thin slice of oak tree; exposed lettuce, sliced
tomatoes and slaughtered carrot were criss-crossed

with a filigree of Heinz salad cream. Taiwo sipped
tasteless piss water from a midget's cup, gripped

his back teeth like a pestle grinding corn in a mortar,
smiled mechanically at the diminutive devil opposite.

Peggy added, 'And what do you *do*, exactly?'
'I'm a welder now but I'm saving my money to study.'

'Oh.' Her elongated vowel suspended itself
over the table like a full colostomy bag. It was the Oh

she'd learnt from the la-di-dahs years ago, omnipotent,
it hovered long after the speaker had gone. Ellen

blurted out, 'Taiwo can quote Shakespeare *and* Shelley.'
Peggy's head revolved like a ventriloquist's dummy,

her eyes mocked Ellen as if she was completely bonkers.
'She does not see me,' Taiwo thought, 'only a coloured.'

Leslie cleared his throat, the throttle of a car starting.
Taiwo looked curiously at this blank page in the story.

'I don't care where you're from, just look after my Ellen.'
Peggy snapped a Digestive, Ellen restrained a giggle,

Taiwo's shoulders dropped four inches. *Beautiful.*
I will remember his words until the day I die.

DISLOYALTY slimes into my kitchen like slugs at night.
Dissension in the ranks. I won't have it, not from anyone.

Mice breed more mice if you don't cheese and snap 'em
so I told Leslie to keep his interfering opinions to himself.

I feel bleached, boiled, scrubbed, rinsed, wrung out
and crucified on a washing line to blanch and stiffen.

I could never love darkie grandchildren. I've *told* her.
But she'll not listen to me or Father Augustus who said

that taking the word of the Lord to the primitives
is one thing, but it's quite another lying down with them.

Chocolate sauce on cod, for Christ's bloomin' sake!
Jacob tried to deflate that silly souffléd head of hers,

explained the vices of racial mixing, the ostracisation,
the children who'd inherit the weaknesses of both races,

who'd bleach their skin white like the American negroes.
Then Violet had a word, surprised her at college, railed on

about the headstrong young who later regret their actions.
Fat lot of good that did, too. Ungrateful little tyke.

As for me, I'm a sandcastle my child's just kicked in.
No, I'm a kettle – screeching, dried out, explosive!

CHAPTER 8

Abbey Wood, London, 1930 –

LESLIE

'WAS BORN in a fog and been in one ever since.'
Leslie was given to say, usually to himself

or Ellen, as they were the only people who listened,
far as he was concerned, not that he was complaining, mind.

Six mornings a week at 3 A.M., when Manton Rd
lay under a mantle of darkness and the night was a cosy

warm, tucked-up, sweet-dreamy sleeping breath,
Leslie wrapped himself up in his woollen overcoat

to begin the hour-long trek from Abbey Wood
to United Dairies in Cemetery Lane, Charlton.

The scuffle of his boots amplified in the empty streets,
until he mounted the last steep hill to the dairy.

He'd see to Sheila first, his ageing mare, whose job
it was to haul both him and his cart in delivering

milk to hundreds of households for their morning
porridge, Shredded Wheat, Kix and hot beverages.

Once out of the dairy gates Leslie transformed himself
into the legendary hero Hopalong Cassidy,

'Enemy of Crime and Cruelty'. Sheila became Topper,
his mighty steed. A Winchester rifle sat on his lap

as he rode the dangerous Texas to Kansas cattle drive,
watchful of rattlesnakes, coyotes and those pesky injuns

before turning back up Cemetery Lane at midday,
feeding his mare lunch, 'Eat up, Sheila, you old sausage',

then catching the tram home for his own.

CAME INTO this world covered in boils,
always been hard of hearing and blind as a bat.

It saved me from conscription but not from persecution
as a child – the number of times I was beaten up.

Was lucky to survive my first few years when death
ran in my family like runny noses ran in others.

Diptheria, Scarlet Fever, Tuberculosis, Meningitis –
five of my grandmother's kids died before the age of two.

The only boy to survive was William Brinkworth: Dad.
A brass machinist down at Woolwich Arsenal.

His dad was William Brinkworth, too: barracks labourer.
Oh yes, admirals, generals, leaders of men and the like.

It's obvious where my driving ambition comes from.
Or lack of it, as Peggy likes to remind me.

She thinks the Brinkworths are as common as muck.
Well, this one hands over his pay packet every week,

thank you Mrs B, a glass of sherry at Christmas
is the extent of my alcoholic tendencies, I've never

looked at another woman (so's anyone would notice),
I help with the domestics, do the gardening fortnightly

and I take Ellen out fishing on the Thamesmead marshes
just to let her slosh around in the water, bless her, or

we push each other in and return home like two strange
but smiling swamp beasts, which winds her mother up

something rotten, especially when we sully No 31
with our scummy clothes and muddy Wellies.

PEGGY'S such a dainty, doll-like little thing,
but for-mee-da-bla, as the Frenchies say. I'd never

dare raise my voice to her. She was so small
at birth she had to be wrapped up in cotton wool.

A whippet of a waist, too, fits nicely round my hands.
So lovely in those pretty floral dresses she makes.

I still look forward to our 'unholy communion', although
I've never seen her peachy beauty unclothed.

Even in darkness she turns her head away.
I've seen her cleavage once or twice. Very nice, too.

But there are things I'd like to do. I am a man,
and I wish she'd leave God outside the bedroom.

Evenings I have a smoke and read the *News Chronicle*
or do the accounts from my rounds. I'm a whizz

at mental arithmetic. It's good to be good at something.
I was rarely in school on account of poor health.

Peggy sews, knits, crochets, listen to the wireless.
Sometimes Mr Hardman from down the road pops in,

or I pootle-off to Mr Walkers for a chin wag.
Peggy doesn't like me gone for long.

I'd like to say it's quieter now Ellen's at college,
but it was just as quiet when she was around.

She's like her father – walks on eggshells.

MY WIFE and my mother can't stand each other.
It's not quite knitting needles drawn at dawn,

or rat poison slipped into cups of afternoon tea,
but if I'm caught between their frozen smiles – it's chilly.

Mother looks inscrutable behind her thick lenses,
like me, I suspect. And hard, which she had to be.

Whereas Peggy finds the Brinkworths too low class,
(like *she's* descended from the Royal House of Windsor

she finds Mother's side, the Wilkenings, a bit too German
I suspect, though she'd never say outright to me

Jacob's German, but he's also a doctor and a Jew,
so exempt from starting two world wars then.

When Mother offers her some pickled beef, sauerkraut
or salt potatoes to rile her (I'm sure), Peggy takes a nibble

and leaves the rest, blaming her 'constitution'.
Won't even partake of delicious Black Forest Gâteaux

which is adored the whole world over.
Mother blames Peggy for taking me away from her.

I was the first boy and sickest. I was, let's say, *clasped*.
Then I went and replaced Mother's spine with Peggy's.

On our weekend visits to the folks, Dad and me
slip out for a smoke and have a joke in the garden

about leaving the battle-axes to start World War Three.
It's all quite ridiculous really because while Mother

is half-German, Peggy herself is half-Irish.

SO WHEN Ellen brought this coloured chap home,
how could I object? He seemed decent enough.

A big, thick-lipped smile like those Negroes have
although the wife tried her hardest to wipe it off him.

Strong white teeth and good health to pass on.
Peggy underestimates our timid little girl, but I don't.

She's smitten. She's stubborn. She'll marry her love.
All that matters to me is that our child is happy.

I doubt I'll be around to hand her over, and Peggy
certainly won't be playing proud mother of the bride.

I'd like to see in my fiftieth year but I doubt it.
Some mornings I can barely make it down the stairs.

When I try to breathe it's like that Sugar Ray Robinson
is doing press-ups on my chest. When I try to walk

electric shocks run up my legs like I'm doing
that jitterbug jive to that swing music Ellen likes.

I'd have loved grandchildren, even picaninny ones.
I can still manage a smoke now and then, on the sly.

I remind me of my German granddad, Louis.
The wheezes, the shakes, the love of smoking.

He paid all my doctor's bills as a child. There was no
National Health Service then. I'd've died but for him.

I won't go against what he stood for. I won't.

CHAPTER 9

LOUIS WILKENING felt like a Teutonic titan,
a warrior colossus bestriding the seas as the *Friedhelm*,

which had brought him safely from Hamburg,
sailed down the Thames towards the Port of London.

He stood up on deck, where he also slept, as the city
where he would make his fortune came into view.

Louis carried youth and hope, impatience and a knife
used to slaughter pigs and slit the throats of chickens,

and he wore clogs carved by the village cobbler
out of a limb of birch found on his dead father's farm but

no jacket, for he had sold it on board to buy bread,
no coppers weighing down the pockets of his trousers,

no photographs of family for none had ever been taken,
no plans to write back for he had never held a pen,

no English words except *Hello*, *Gutbye* and *How you are?*
no doubts about the future when starvation was the past.

When the *Friedhelm* dropped anchor at Royal Victoria Dock
so too did his heart – there was no looking back.

A young outlander determined to conquer England,
Louis rolled up his sleeves to look for work.

ROBBED of his clogs, rats chewed his toes, bats
hung upside down from the eaves of the wharf's arches,

a battalion of lice squirmed in his scalp, he cursed,
clambered up, surveyed the stinking, urine-stained

mass of human despair escaping the rain: mothers,
babies, children of the streets, cripples, drunks,

the insane, blind, ancient, contagious, dying, dead.
He had barely slept in weeks, *not safe*, but his eyes

kept closing. He could do anything, he'd begged
bosses with his eyes, except – speak the language.

He stole a bagel, brandy-ball, penny pie,
and one heaven-sent slice of mouth-watering spiced cake.

In the end he succumbed to the oldest trade
and sold himself – for three beers in a tavern.

Welcome to London, Louis.
Welcome to England, your Garden of Eden.

THE ASYLUM for the Houseless Poor
slid back the bolts of its great oak doors to Louis

and his ilk only when morning threatened to find each one
a glassy-eyed, foetal-shaped block of ice.

Africans, Chinamen, Lascars, Irish, Scots, English –
the pauperised in the largest city in the world.

Close to the blazing stove Louis felt his bones thaw,
with hot tea inside full sentences formed in his mind,

for the first time in weeks he was lucid.
From an old German seaman at his side, he took advice.

This was an angry, savage, hungry city, he was told,
where very few struck gold. *Stick to your own.*

The German Society of Benevolence shaved the vermin
from his head, set his hair and foul clothes alight

(how he sobbed when his humilation turned to ash),
doused him in a hot tub, donated hosen, shirt, cap, jacket,

a grease-and-beef sandwich for supper and a blanket
smelling of soda and the promise of night's bliss.

Next morning he was sent to a German sugar bakery
in Whitechapel – to earn his daily bread.

LOUIS

SUGAR BAKING is ze shit vurk of ze devil.
Two years I vurk like pig in schob not fit for monkey.

It arrives on river from Vest Indies looking like dung,
und leaves boiling house sparkling vhite.

I slave in dark cellar und put sugar liquor
in bucket vhich is back breaking und den I run

across cellar to put in basin vhere sugar is bleached, driet out,
und den I shovel it into fucking sugar mountain.

'Time is money, *Herren*,' Master Bumface Kayser say.
We pait piecevork. 'Too slow no dough!' he shout.

Sometimes ve vurk from 3 in mornink to 8 at evenink.
Vages more vurse than Irish hod carrier, even.

Ze air is foggy, schmoking und so hot I can't breaze.
Machine make noise all damnt time und make me deaf.

Sugar make me sick until I don't schmell no more.
Sugar make me sick until I don't taste no more.

Sugar schlop from pail und burn bad on my schkin.
Effery day sveat. Vet! Sveat! Vet! Sveat! Vet! *Scheisse!*

Master giffe uz beer to keep goink, but it make me sick.
Ve vorking-men Germens are schkum of London.

English say Germens haffe no morals und drink too much.
I vill proof them wronk. I am good man, yes, Man!

My two years finish so eat *scheisse*, Herr Miser-Kayser.
Today I am tventy year old. Tomorrow I get new schob.

ICH BIN EIN Master Baker, Louis would proudly declare
years later, twisting the ram's horns of his moustache,

smoothing down his crisp baker's apron or inhaling
on his Filet St Omer pipe from Fortnum & Masons,

for he had acquired a taste for the finer things in life.
After an apprenticeship with Brummerhoop & Sons,

he'd set himself up across the Thames with a barrow
to call his own in the garrison town of Woolwich.

Home was a room in Hog Lane in the Dusthole slums
down by the river but he'd traipsed the town battling

rain, snow storms, ice and exhaustion dreaming,
of the shop front that would one day bear his name.

At No 71 Henry Street on South Watson's Wharf,
Wilkenings sold plaited loaves, fragrant cinnamon buns,

scrumptious sweet bread with a glaze of honey.
His soft crullers were a melt-in-the-mouth delight

and he made pumpernickel especially for his compatriots
who knew the benefits of a good morning dump.

With the purchase of No 72 he was ready, finally,
to find a lady companion and start a clan.

LOUIS

EDWIN and George Huxtable, my chums next door
pop over with ale to go with my pork sausages,

frog march me to fashionable dances to find wife.
When I try Blind Man's Buff I charge across floor

like I am with bayonet in battle, make my dancing
partner Gladys fall over and graze her knee

and everyone thinks I am intoxicated tosspot.
When I see Gladys at dance in golden gown with frills

like curtains, with bustle, tight bodice, moving bosoms
and strong bread-kneading shoulders exposed,

chestnut hair all curled up like glazed pastry rings
I know this comely girl will make healthy babies for me.

She does not mind I look like jackass when dance.
She does not mind I trip over words like furniture.
She does not mind I look at her feet when I speak.
She does not mind when I ask her to be my bride.

I married Gladys, of Islington, County of Middlesex,
in ceremony in Woolwich, County of Kent,
at 11 A.M. in the morning on the 19th day of July, 1871.

(I will be her 'Louis Lambkins' until the day I die.)

A MAN is not a man until he has produced sons.
A woman is not a woman until she makes babies.

1872 – a girl, Louisa: I did not show disappointment.
1873 – a boy, Frederick: he will follow in my footsteps.
1874 – a girl, Lydia: I pray second son soon comes.
1876 – a girl, Emily: she did not stay with us for long.
1878 – a boy, Caleb: neither did he.
1879 – a girl, Caroline-Ada: my wife is overjoyed.
1883 – a girl, Florence: why am I being punished?
(Gladys pleads we give up, but I will not be defeated.)
1890 – a boy, Harry: after seventeen years failing!
1891 – a boy, Arthur: Okay, Gladys, we stop now.

How English I have become with my English love,
and blood, whose native tongue is not of my own.

This is my country now. I have built my home.
My wife raises our stock to be obedient and hygienic,

she helps out in the bakery when housework
is completed to highest possible standards.

I am lately Deputy President of the Association of Bakers
(Kent Region). I have purchased No 76 for expansion

and bought a phonograph for the back parlour.
Gladys plays that *ta ra ra boom dee-yay* nonsense.

I prefer Ludwig Van Beethoven and, once a year,
hail a carriage to Blackheath Conservatoire, alone.

GLADYS DREAMS of a Royal Doulton flushing toilet.
I dream Harry and Arthur will enter my business.

She retorts they'll do as they please, likely.
Wife's got lippy of late. I should slap her,

but she'll only slap my face harder, *likely*.
Yet still we dream of sweet dotage together.

The German Colony in Woolwich is growing,
but the land they left behind is not one I remember –

they are more stranger than compatriot, alas.
So many weddings we have had: Louisa to Sidney,

Overlooker of Explosives at the Arsenal.
Frederick to Mary from Scotland (He works at my side.)

Lydia to Francis Bickerstaff, Spirit Merchant up
at Charlton Village. Caroline to William Brinkworth,

Brass Machinist at the Arsenal. (Not the brightest catch
in town but neither, God forgives me, is she.)

How my lovely lady wife produced such a plain,
surly child beggars my belief. Their boy Leslie

is an ailing thing. It is my duty to keep him alive.
Our Florence emigrated with Wilfrid to Australia,

which cracked open her mother's heart, and mine.
Saturdays I take youngest boys to watch

Woolwich Arsenal get beaten. Second-rate losers.
The Gunners, that is, not my sons.

WHEN HOARDINGS declare war with Germany
I thank God I am Naturalised Citizen not 'Enemy Alien'.

Still – locals cross the road at my approach,
rumour I am one of the Kaiser's despised spies,

degrade my shutters with 'GO HOME FILTHY HUN!',
shout 'Traitor!' to harass my loyal customers

so that my sweet bread hardens into stale bricks
and for first time ever my ovens get stone cold.

(*They are my neighbours.*
Over 50 years.
I am known.)

When a submarine torpedoed the *Lusitania*,
I am as furious as any other upstanding person

and curse those bastards making lambs to slaughter, but –
LOCK THEM ALL UP! screams the *Daily Sketch*;

German businesses are burnt down, we are sacked,
refused service, men beaten up, daschunds stoned,

police even search my home for carrier pigeons!
Soon all German males incarcerated on Isle of Man

where they eat birds and miss their wives and children.
By end of the war 30,000 are deported.

ONE STICKY summer's night Woolwich seethed
after Zeppelin bombers had bombarded the Arsenal

with explosions which reverberated for miles,
and the tide of the Thames had swollen to overflowing,

and a mob emerged from The Gunmakers Arms
on the rampage and converged on Wilkenings,

their faces bulbous knots, their voices crushed glass,
with rocks gripped in reddened fists they smashed

the bakery windows, raided the premises and trashed it
while Louis, who'd just extinguished his bedside lamp

and crawled underneath the sheet to cuddle Gladys,
stumbled downstairs in his stripy nightshirt – horrified.

When they left he collapsed on a carpet of flour,
shattered glass, scattered coal, smeared faeces, and cried.

The next day he boarded up shop. Later it was sold.
He put everything in crates and packed up his heart.

He moved up to Plumstead – to No 63 Griffin Road.
And when the heart of his beloved Gladys stopped,

he crawled into the back parlour, and just sat there
day and night, in darkness, alone.

I AM A MAN not a nation, Louis was given to say
on the rare occasion he had conversations.

He took to playing Wagner so loud the neighbours
complained but he didn't give a damn about them,

playing *Ride of the Valkyries* over and over again.
At No 63 Griffin Road the curtains were closed.

He sat in the parlour puffing on his Filet St Omer pipe,
buried in mountains of smoke, his once-erect back

curved and shrank and his lungs struggled to expand.
His grandson Leslie visited after school,

to sit with the man who had saved his life,
who told him to treat people as singular, not plural,

and to play his 'chest close to his cards'.
Louis never spoke of how Frederick had hung himself

soon after coming home from the trenches,
how shell-shocked Arthur still couldn't find work,

nor Harry who lost his fishmongers when he signed up.
A year after the Treaty of Versailles was signed,

Louis was buried in a plot next to Gladys in a corner
of Woolwich – which would be forever – foreign.

PART TWO

CHAPTER 10

TAIWO

'ELLIE, marry me soon. You are of age now.
Your mama will either cease this nonsense or disown you,

but at least she will stop dousing you with water
then running a live electric wire over your body.

These British think they are so superior to coloureds,
they believe those stupid Tarzan films from America.

To me they are cardboard people with chessboard minds.
You do not see how they sneer at me in the street?

Sweet Ellie, you do not see the evil in this world.
That is why I love you. You are spring water.'

He pulled her towards him as if leading her to waltz.
She curled into his chest with feline fluidity,

all angst dissipated against his warm wool sweater.
She undid the clip which imprisoned her auburn curls

in a sweeping French knot on her head, the red flush
of desire prickled her gooseberry flesh each time

his hands swept down her arms. She floated, tensionless,
on water, safe, bobbing, open to the swirl of gravity.

Then her mind opened. It was dark. Time to go back
to college and prepare for her wedding.

SNOWFLAKES sprinkled down that cold Christmas Eve,
anointed Ellen's dark-green and cherry-red costume,

vanished in the gravel drive of Sacred Heart Church
where, linked with Taiwo in his Moss Bros suit,

she smiled into the winking eye of a black box camera,
as excitedly they albumed their chiaroscuro union.

'Marry in red, wish you were dead!' was Peggy's
parting arrow the day before, but Ellen watched it

fall to the ground as confetti sprayed over the joyous two
from the waving hands of their cheering friends, before

they all tumbled into a limo and several old bangers
and headed for a slap-up of rice, stew, cakes and beer.

'A man's happiest day, is it not? Yes, it is, truly, indeed.
I have beaten the demons and married my beloved.

Ah, if only Mama were here to see her handsome son.
Would she approve? I suspect she too would be trouble.

So, it's time to make a new life with a wife and children.
Today joy fills me like twenty beers but still I think

of Kehinde. I've added another layer she'll never know.
Today I search her eyes like pebbles in a lake.

TAIWO/ELLEN

My hands cup two creamy breasts,
I feel their heaviness, they ripple when I jig them.

The muscles of a boxer, a tiny waist, enviable,
round buttocks so hard they slip when pinched.

I spread her thighs, she goes pink, they are smooth,
thick brown hair covers her juicy pussy. Ruff! Ruff!

His penis grows, I find the tip and circle it,
his hardness feels so strong I almost fear it.

Her mouth is fresh and shy, my tongue pokes about.
I want my stick in there, to be lollipopped.

He runs his long fingers through me. I gasp.
Is it wrong to enjoy this? I feel so embarrassed.

I gather the folds on her spine as I massage her back.
She is all flesh, comforting. I drown in her.

His stomach is so flat, he can't possibly eat enough.
He leads me back to his thing, I stroke it like a cat.

I chew and pull her nipples as if to drink from them.
They flop on my face, I want to gobble them up.

He grabs my buttocks as if kneading dough,
then takes my breasts as if milking a cow.

I can't wait, I must plunge into her immediately,
I put it in while kissing her so she is distracted.

My cry is muffled by his tongue but he is gentle lion,
he fills my inner walls and sweat pours off him.

I scream out once, twice, thrice, then explode.
I imagine all those babies inside me. I love him.

CHAPTER 11

LARA

I SHOT into creation as sperm from my father's penis,
slept in my mother's womb for eight months and ten days

then slid out her dilated hole as if on a muddy slide.
My entry to this island was messy, impatient and dramatic.

I was born May twenty-eight, the year Nineteen Sixty-two,
when England was fast asleep and the moon rose,

a luminescent sickle in a sky of heaving indigo waves;
when a gloved hand smacked my wrinkled bum I bawled

air into activated lungs, grieving the sea I'd left behind.
They named me Omolara 'the family are like water',

and my crumpled mother wept joy at my perfection
for amid all the soup, snot and chord I was proportioned:

two arms, legs, eyes, one nose, ten fingers and toes.
My frayed father expelled smoke on the quiet landing

while the midwife mopped my dishevelled mother.
Juliana, Ginevra and Quentin, my siblings three, snoozed

in pastel cots upstairs, innocent of my determined arrival.
I entered this world with everything, nothing, and as one

who feels watched every second, every minute, every hour.

I GOT two big googly eyes an' tufty hair
an' I a fat little sugar-sweetie-honey-bunch.

'Honeybunch!' my mammy gurgles, an' then she
squeezes my cheeks. 'Look, just like two cushions',

an' I laugh 'cos I like my mammy to play with me.
My big sister Juliana bounces me on her knee,

'Lara, you're my best doll, you know.' She holds
me tightly so's I don' fall flat on my face an'

I want to crawl down the hall to the door but when
I struggle from her arms I tumble down an' she says,

'Don't cry, Lara. There, there, let me kiss it better.'
I like my big brother Quentin best 'cos he pulls

funny faces and does silly dances and tickles
me until I giggle an' giggle an' dribble all over.

When my daddy comes home from work I want
him to pick me up an' hold me tight but he jus' pats

my head and goes downstairs to cook his dinner.
I cry when he tells me off 'cos his voice is angry.

'Lara! You bad, bad girl! You bad-bad-bad-bad girl!'
All the people make words so fast I have to run

and run in my head an try to catch them.
I got a new baby brother now so my mammy is busy.

I cuddle my teddy when I go sleep at night.

A FIZZY-EYED beauty with creamy skin, Juliana,
our eldest, instantly stitched the seeping wound diseasing

my parents and Nana, who, on seeing this caramel delight
was mollified, fell uncontrollably in love with her.

No thick-lipped Negroid child was this but a paler hybrid
and Nana, who'd expected a Taiwo replica, worshipped her.

Not so Dora and Jacob, who chose the invisible life
postwar, in a salubrious set-back in upmarket Snaresbrook,

where they raised two sons who were middle-classed –
Ellen's letters, cards and photographs went unanswered.

Ginevra followed a year later, Quentin fast behind.
After me came Fabian, Laetitia, Ladipo and young Kenelm.

Eight embryos ballooned into children in ten busy years,
my mother's soul-saving business was rapidly expanding.

I was born at 286 Westmount Road, Eltham, the deposit
a belated gift from Nana, though her olive wand,

spiked with the thorns of rose bushes, was conditional:
no lodgers should supplement their income, so Daddy

shelved his studies in order to greet the mortgage.
Then, when we were spilling out of every room

like stuffed toys crammed into a tiny box, we moved
to Woolwich, and room for a growing tribe.

LARA

NO 173 Eglinton Road, 'Atlantico', sits like a fat Victorian
dolls' house on its own high land behind Nightingale Vale

which rolls towards the wasteland of Woolwich Common.
Bland houses, shops, parks and imposing army façades

fan up and out from the River Thames which sulks
like a dirty industrial puddle down by the old Arsenal.

Atlantico was part of Notre Dame Convent next door,
though all links were severed many decades before.

Four staircases climb the basement to attic bedrooms
via splintery wooden stairs and sweeping walnut banisters.

The garden slopes like an untended terraced field citizened
by two of apple, pear, sweet and sour cherry trees.

A wood lurks at the bottom, home to foxes and owls.
Next door slow nuns stoop, black bats in midsummer sun,

gathering fruit into baskets, offering us wild strawberries
while we pick cooking apples for their chunky jams.

An alley skulks down the garden's exposed right side;
a garage, plastered to Atlantico's torso, is an artificial limb;

huge Catholic windows stand watch over the distant Thames
which despatches mist and fog horns on grey mornings.

Sprawling, bedraggled, it is a wild mix of town and country.

IF I WERE a poet, Ellen muses, I'd say life's a mangle,
squeezing every last drop out of me till I'm bloodless.

My arms are either full of babies, shopping, food,
or steeped in bowls of soapy water – flakes and liquid.

Saturday nights are action-packed. It's all Go! Go! Go!
down at my psychedelic disco. I barely catch my breath.

First four hours I bathe, comb and file my grubby eight,
then pop their curly tops into bed, bunks and cots.

Just as the evening play comes on telly and a piping cup
of tea seeps and tingles through my bloodstream,

I trot down to the kitchen sink, roll up my sleeves to erase
all childhood stains from tops, bottoms and all-in-ones.

The whites go into a huge pail on the stove to dissolve
dirt and fill my house with the aroma of boiling cotton.

I make intimate, passionate love with some hard green soap,
seducing woollens, synthetics and coloured cottons.

By 10.30 I'm done but it's no Saturday night movie for me.
My final flirtation is with an iron and ironing board,

a week's ironing does not get done by fairies in the night.
By 12 the party's over and I'm ready to collapse, comatose.

Sleep inevitably takes me to a paradise Greek island
but just as I nod off my youngest starts screaming.

A CATS' CHORUS rains onto corrugated dustbins
as autumn's first wind howls around Atlantico's girth.

Lara kneels, face squashed against the steamy window
of the playroom, deserted by her siblings who've

tripped, leapt and elbowed down to tea in a whirlwind gallop.
In the front garden through the blur of splattering rain

she sees people watching her, young, old, so strange,
sitting motionless in a semi-circle on the grass,

lips unmoving but eyes alive with the singing of song:
'Lara kiss, Lara kiss, we love you always, Lara kiss.'

Lara holds her breath, screws her eyes shut then opens
them to nothing but bruised grass and a whisper of a tune.

'Lara! Get down here this minute. *Whatever* are up to?'
'I'm coming, Mummy,' she descends the wooden stairs

to take her place on the plastic-flowered kitchen table.
'Mummy, I saw Daddy People in the garden singing me.'

'Yes, and pigs might fly. Now eat your tea before I eat you.'
'I *did*!' she screeched, then sat pushing out her bottom lip.

Ellen raised her eyes to the ceiling, this fourth child of hers
was just the limit at times. Too fanciful, too boisterous

and too much silly imagination for her own good.
The child was too old for this malarkey. It had to stop.

CHAPTER 11

DAWN released London from anonymous night,
spires, bridges, monuments, a silver flash of Thames

emerged from darkness under the insipid eyes
of giraffes which lined the deserted embankments.

Battersea Power Station loomed incongruous, Peruvian
Temple of Energy, magnetising bleary-eyed men

who approached it, the spokes of a wheel to its hub.
Cloth cap, donkey jacket, dungarees, steel-toed boots

adorned men who will work iron, levers, pistons
until twilight diffuses the city skyline opaque again.

Taiwo double-decker dreamed his way to Battersea
each morning, long before the wife and progeny stirred.

Life is a boxing ring with no referee, judge or prize.
How I tire of defending my right to exist on these
great British isles. How I ache with invisible bruises.
How I long to saunter casually down the road
without tensing my stomach muscles, ready for foes.
Hey, what a speech. I will write a play. One to rival
Saint Joan. 'The Tired Boxer' by Taiwo da Costa,
the brilliant new Bernard Shaw from the colonies.
Ah, if only. First to provide for my brood in a job
where my imagination dies and my soul suffocates.

TAIWO

MY CHILDREN will not swim in a lake of lost dreams,
with discipline they will flourish in my new republic.

I line my little army up for two important reasons,
the first – to greet people to the house, the second –

when they are so bad that punishment is due:
a broken window, ripped sofa, money missing.

I put Juliana at the head, then age down to Kenelm,
make them stand still until they admit their crime.

With so many they think they can fool their daddy,
but I can wait forever, eat dinner, read the paper,

until the culprits own up and are suitably chastised.
If not, they all make friends with my wooden spoon.

'Left hands out,' I order, then work my way down.
The seniors get 15 strokes, the youngest a mere tap.

Their lips tremble, they push back crocodile tears.
If the boys cry, I hit harder. Weakness is not a male asset.

Finally, dismissed, they troop out of the kitchen.
'Don't hit them, Taiwo,' Ellen moans. She is too soft.

I will not have it. I know how to raise my children.
This is a harsh, harsh world. They will be prepared.

I must show them the ropes, so to speak.

THE KEY turned. The front door.
Lara's throat dehydrated, saliva syringed down

her windpipe. Her tummy a tumble-dryer, thrashed.
Her heart became a man's hobnail boot kicking,

trying to break through the delicate ribs of her chest.
She tried to outstare the television. If she blinked

water would free up, spill out of the sockets, be seen.
The tribe sat, entranced by *The Magic Roundabout.*

Thudded feet, the hall's floorboards groaned, then
the Best Room door opened and Taiwo boomed in,

his voice shuddering, gravely, laden with authority.
They held their breaths, turned, synchronised

like clockwork toys, chimed, 'Good evening, Daddy,'
in tinkling voices. Taiwo's boots descended the stairs.

Lara tried to breathe evenly but spluttered, coughed.
Her stomach was a ripe watermelon now waiting

for a machete to swoop from above and split it.
Taiwo's voice vibrated up through the kitchen ceiling,

he always sounded angry, even when not.
His voice rumbled, was raised, went silent.

LARA

HE CALLED me downstairs, potatoes were boiling,
sausages popped in a pan, the radio was nattering.

'Go and empty the rubbish.' I duly obeyed.
I was a good girl really, would I be let off, this time?

The brown leather belt which hung by the window
was missing, this was serious, belt not spoon.

'Get over here.' I scurried over, face neutral,
the distinction between fear and pain dissolved.

'Have I told you not to play in the street?
Discipline,' he growled, 'Disss-i-ppaaa-lin.'

Buckle wrapped around knuckles, arm raised,
the first lash left my palm numb and smarting,

the second burned as if rubbed with stinging nettles,
the third felt like a cheese grater had shaved my skin,

by the tenth raw lacerations were dipped in vinegar.
I ground my teeth, tried to look intensely sorry,

my red pulsating hand puffed up like a boxing glove.
Tears were either a blessing or a curse with my father.

I unblocked a few drops, miraculously he stopped.
My feet made sure the stairs did not creak,

I immersed myself in my eiderdown with muted tears.
Fear was preferable to pain, until the next time.

I WANT Mummy Cake! I want Daddy Cake!
the triblings squealed when Ellen lay coveted treats,

chocolate and lemon Swiss rolls, on the kitchen table.
Tea time was usually one lettuce leaf per child, half

a tom, beetroot, cress and Mother's Pride sliced.
Ellen studied nutrition so the tribe thrived on pennies,

worked it out down to the last vitamin and mineral.
Fridays were fish and chips, Saturdays fried liver,

Sundays – traditional roast or Daddy's special dinner,
beef pepper stew and rice with optional gooey okra.

Once old enough the children were doing the dishes,
helping with the shopping, cleaning the house Saturdays.

Summertime Taiwo sent them into the jungle
with shears to level grass taller than themselves

while Ellen served squash at hot and sticky intervals.
Taiwo thought his little army was shaping up nicely.

Peggy spent winters crotcheting multi-coloured blankets,
knitting scarves, jumpers, making summer dresses.

She scoured department stores for bargain furniture
and put by weekly to buy them shoes from Clarks.

She never made forays to No 173 Eglinton Road
but every Sunday two of her grandchildren traipsed

with Ellen to tea at their grandmothers, leaving
a sixpence, boiled sweets and several cakes richer.

BY THE SLOPING woods daffodils bloom in the spring sun,
Lara's birthday, toffee child in yellow dress, ruched,

gathered, bowed, dances at the garden's edge, where
the woods begin, her magic wand – a branch – pirouettes

the air, summons the Daddy People to appear,
phantoms perched in trees like owls, smiling, singing.

She spins on white sandals, giggles, giddy spinning top,
admires her new ankle socks fringed with white lace.

Suddenly, shocking the spring air, a missile hurtles
down, 'Eenaaaarrrf!' Taiwo's vibrato, basso profoundo,

flies down before him. 'Are you deranged, eh?'
He snatches the wand from her hand, breaks it in two.

Milk comes unexpectedly, dangerously, nay recklessly
to the boil. 'I was talking to the Daddy People!'

she shouts back, stamping her feet, 'Nosy Parker!'
Oh little piggy, who is going to eat you for dinner.

Incredulous he dances barefoot on burning coals.
'What? How dare you!', louder, 'Bend over!'

Lara bears nine hard strokes from the broken wand,
runs up the garden an inferno of raging hysteria.

That night in bed she called the Daddy People to her,
said farewell, and willed them away forever.

NOTRE DAME'S regime was run by Mother Superior,
a bloated red-veined matriarch hidden behind thick

specs, swathed in a voluminous black habit, who'd
patrol the school's stark polished corridors

to catch an errant child, late, running, or chewing gum.
Leaving home a minute before the clock hit nine,

Lara and Co., in berets, hats, blazers, tumbled out
their rusting gate straight into the convent's biblical one

as pupils filed silently into the chapel for Mass.
Taiwo was pleased that he'd haggled for a bargain.

'A job lot, like,' he'd convinced Mother Superior,
so the da Costa fees to the school were at a discount.

For years he did overtime to meet the payments.
Religiously instructed every morning and country-danced

on Tuesdays Lara was three R'd the rest of the week,
digesting pease pudding and tapioca at dinner time.

'Think of the starving children in Africa,' the nuns
berated until their charges' plates were scraped clean.

Fat Sister Nicodemus and six-footer Sister Mary Paul
headed the Juniors and Seniors with staccato wrists

ready to ruler-rap the knuckles of talkative children.
From the cloisters of school and the confines of home,

Lara inhaled fear masquerading as air.

LARA

Nineteen Sixty-seven, our father is crying.
We sneak outside, peer through the kitchen window,

watch him heave, blow his nose, raises his head
Mummy holds his hand, gives him toilet paper.

We try to be quiet, jostle for a better view. Ladipo whines.
I push him. 'Shush. Quiet you two!' Fabian snaps.

We settle, watching. 'He's crying!' says Kenelm.
'Makes a change,' says Quentin.

Juliana creeps up behind us, hisses, 'Stop spying!'
We bristle but do not budge. 'Anyway,' she says,

'I know why he's currently emotionally incapacitated.'
She relishes the status her long words give her,

runs down the garden, jumps on the apple tree swing,
then pushes off. We pause, scramble after her.

'You're lying,' Ginevra challenges. / 'Oh no, I'm noh-oht,'
Juliana sing-songs, swings away, grins between two Heidi plaits,

enunciates slowly, 'Well, if you really must know,
his mother died two weeks ago but he just got the letter.'

I feel queasy. Do I have to feel sorry for him then?
'All right, kiddiwinks, go inside and wash. Bedtime.

Go on!' Juliana orders, but falters, her power expended.
Our eyes mock. I cross my arms. Our feet grow roots.

'Hop it!' she shouts, but we hear the plea in her voice.
'Mummy's orders. Scram!' We saunter up to the house.

111

I AM A STRONG MAN but pain is a warrior too.
The pit I build for grief this time will be infinite.
Be strong, Taiwo, your life depends on it.

A letter arrived this morning from Nigeria.
The sea carried it here. She died May five,
went midday, her last breath, 'Taiwo, Taiwo',
like a mantra she kept calling him, her boy,
she could not get over losing him to England.

All gone now – Baba, Papa, Mama, Kehinde.
How will I survive in this refrigerator?
I must erase their memory.

They are waiting for him but we have no money.
He won't talk to me, give voice to his thoughts,
but thank God he is crying and how, for the first
time, I see my husband broken down.

I must return prosperous or be shamed.
You cannot go to Europe and return a poor man.
When the roots of a tree die, its seeds are re-born.
My children are my seed. This is home now.

CHAPTER 12

AN EMERALD Raleigh cycled through Lara's childhood,
ever new, three gears, she rode her imagination

around the garden for hours, hop, push, skip on, skip on,
pretending to freewheel down country hills

or puff victorious in the Children's Olympics.
Expeditions in books borrowed from the library

liberated her from the enclosure of Eglinton Road,
for when fog vaporised the dark, lamp-lit street,

she became the beautiful Maisie in *The Orphan Girl*,
a story she'd made up, just like Dickens: poor, she

was pale, parentless, persecuted, pitiful, plebeian,
puny, poxy, proud, pensive, polioed, placid,

powerless, pathetic, piss-wet and shivering outside
the mansions of 'them rich oose Christmas trees

dripped diamonds and oose turkeys glittered gold'.
And when snow transformed Lara's hilly vista, she

escaped first light, donned duffel coat, balaclava,
mittens, struggled to open the basement's frozen

lock and enter the Antarctic as Captain Scott,
a brave lone figure conquering the desolate white.

She ceremoniously stuck a stick in the snow, for England,
then became self-conscious, searched the windows

for a sibling laughing. Nothing stirred, not even wind.
Cold, she dashed back to the gas fires of home.

LARA'S SKIN oozed honey in late summer's oven,
lounging amid triffid grass where dandelions fainted.

Diseased apples were decimated by maggots, wasps
sucked the sugar of bleeding cherries. She languorously

gorged purple flesh, her lips stained Midnight Mauve.
Lara's sepia cheeks rouged with the heat of summer,

sunk into a ripped deck chair, she bathed, tired
of the school holidays, six weeks down, two to go.

What was the sea like? she wondered. 'All blue and grey,'
Peggy told her, 'but the beach makes your toes messy.'

Face full on to the sun, its strokes painted her a rusty brown
until sun-drunk, she stumbled inside. 'Look, I've a sun tan.'

'Don't be silly, dear,' Ellen mumbled, rolling thick pastry.
Three at a time she vaulted the stairs, passing Fabian.

'Jagger-lips!' he teased, sliding down the banister
out of her reach. 'Watusi-head!' she retaliated loudly,

reaching her attic bedroom and slamming the door.
She studied her lips in the mirror. They weren't too big,

not like her father's or that Nat King Cole man
whose boring *Mona Lisa* drifted up the stairs at night.

Still, she'd suck them in from now on, just in case.

TANK TOPS, Curly Wurlys, blue mascara, Top 20,
T. Rex, Jackson 5, Bowie, Slade, the Sweet, the 70s

spun Lara into the kaleidoscope of teeny bop,
at Eltham Hill Girls she torpedoed chewing gum

on entering, hitched her skirt on exiting, tissue-padded
her non-existents in the upstairs loo, and choked

over smoke at lunchtime behind the Jubilee Gardens.
Lacrosse, rounders, tennis, hockey, swimming, relay

rotated weekly with maths, physics, history, Latin et al,
ad infinitum, timetabled to inject seeds of academia

into hormonal cells. Lara (now La), and Susie (aka Soos),
blooded a pin-prick bond forged on a passion for boys,

pop, clothes and garrulous babble. Shorn playing fields
lolled from tennis courts to the slopes of Eltham Green,

stunted herbaceous borders prettified the red-brick exterior,
inside its panelled walls inhaled school dinners,

the distinctive odour of years of mush and slop.
Five hundred blue-beret'd, pre and après pubescents

descended the stern gates to the ivy-clad grammar.
Lara da Costa, hopping off the 161 from Woolwich, only

child of discernible colour, did not notice her difference,
camouflaged by her uniform and the nattering swarm

of pink-flushed, off-white, excitable girlies.

'WANNA BITE, Soos? Wanna bite, La?'
Madeline, third member of the triumvirate, slouched in,

brandishing a decapitated Topic and two auburn plaits.
'No, ta. You'll get spots if you eat sweets,' Susie tutted.

'I don't care if I do!' Madeline plonked herself on a bench,
flung beefy shot-putter legs onto a desk, studied Susie

putting on Lypsil with the affectation of applying lipstick.
'Your lips are so luscious, Soos. Mine are too thin, see?'

She pouted, accentuating her trout's lips. 'I know, Mad.
Mine are called cupid lips or rosebud or summing.'

Lara wondered what was so special about Susie's lips,
same size as hers and shape, just a different colour.

'And you've nice long legs, Soos. Look at my fat stumps.'
Madeline snorted. 'Yuk. Hey, I've got a great idea.

You two have a Miss Lovely Legs Competition.
I read in a mag that you put your feet together, insert

a penny near your whatsit, (they giggled), and if it slots in
you've got perfect legs. You first, Soos. Yeees. Perfect.

Now you, La. Nope, it won't go through at all. Soreee.'
Lara wanted to cry, her legs were all right before,

now she knew they weren't. She masked it, joined
the other two prancing around the room chanting,

'Susie's Miss Lovely Legs! Susie's Miss Lovely Legs!'

'WISH I HAD hair like yours, Soos. It's so nice.'
'Yeh, it's long but it goes like haywire at night, La.

I used to scream like hell in the mornings. Truly!'
Theatrically Susie tossed back her yellow mane,

brushed it effortlessly. 'Mum says it's my crowning glory.'
She jumped off the desk in the empty classroom, bent

over, hair dropped like a waterfall, she back-combed it.
What was it like to see your hair in front of you, Lara

wondered. All she could do with hers was part it down
the middle and stick in stupid pins so it stayed put.

She hated her hair, couldn't even fit the school beret on,
it just bounced off. As for the boater – forget it.

'Yours is so soft and bouncy, Lara.' Susie patted her head.
'See, just like a sponge. Amazing.' A surf of anger surged

through Lara at her own hair. If only Susie knew how hard
it was to comb though its trillion stubborn tangles.

'Course, I have to wash mine every day else it gets greasy.
Dad says blondes have more fun but it's such a drag. Truly!'

The mane was bunched up for split-end inspection,
released, flicked over her right shoulder, shaken out,

flicked over her left shoulder, shaken out.
Susie peered intensely at Lara's hair, said solemnly.

'You do wash your hair, don't you, La?' She sighed at Lara's
affirmative nod. 'Good.' She ruffled her mane.

'What's up, Lara? C'mon, it might never happen.'

BENEATH the squawking eaves of her attic retreat,
before Laetitia appeared for bed and the customary row,

Lara sought to resolve the issue of her springy hedge;
slender hands dived into her chest of drawers, quickly

extracted her long, red-ribbed cardy, placed it excitedly
over her head so it fell, equally either side, like hair.

But the wardrobe's oblong mirror muttered
'Silly billy,' her head was too bulky underneath.

What to do? She dug out her white swimming cap,
squeezed her abundance into it, donned red cardy again,

but the mirror cringed 'Wrong colour,' it yelled, 'yellow.'
Surreptitiously, Lara the cat burglar, tippy-toed downstairs,

tensing at every Victorian tell-tale squeak. She sneaked
into her parent's bedroom, sought her mother's yellow

cardigan, long, soft, lambswool, then, lightfoot as a spider,
snuck back upstairs, carefully placed the yellow hair

on her swimming head, held breath, 1, 2, 3, Hey Presto!,
to the magic circle she'd go for she was now a blonde.

She experimented, flicked it to the right, shook it out,
flicked it to the left, shook it out, skipped, danced,

read a book so it fell over her face, tossed it back.
Only when Laetitia's slippered feet creaked the landing,

did she snatch it all off, hurry to her desk,
grab her recorder, and play *Greensleeves*, innocently.

'WHERE'RE'YOU from, La?' Susie suddenly asked
one lunch break on the playing fields. 'Woolwich.'

'No, silly, where're'you from, y'know, originally?'
'If you really must know I was born in Eltham, actually.'

'My dad says you must be from Jamaica,' Susie insisted.
'I'm not Jamaican. I'm English.' / 'Then why are you coloured?'

Lara's heart shuddered, she felt humiliated, so angry.
'Look, my father's Nigerian, my mother's English, all right?'

'Oh, so you're half-caste.' Lara tore at the grass in silence.
'Where's Nigeria then, is it near Jamaica?' / 'It's in Africa.'

'Where's Africa exactly?' / 'How should I know, I don't
bloody well live there, do I?' / 'Is your Dad from the jungle?'

That was it. Lara sprang up, brushed grass off her skirt,
pulled up her socks, flung her satchel over her shoulder,

stormed off. Susie ran after her. 'What's the matter, Lara?'
'You're bloody rude, that's the matter.' Tears were edging

their way out, blurred she strode on. 'Well he could be
from the jungle, couldn't he?' Susie looked perplexed,

Lara felt so stupid blubbing in public. 'Look, I didn't mean
to hurt you, honest. I'm really sorry. Anyway, as far

as I'm concerned you're nearly white, all right? And I *adore*
your hair, it's just like a Brillo pad. Truly!' Lara stopped,

smiled, sighed, said, 'Race you to the tuck shop.
Last one there buys a packet of salt and vinegar',

'YOU DIDN'T do it with him, did you?'
'What d'ya think I did, play musical chairs?'

'Oh my God. You did it. You lost it.' Lara's head yo-yoed
amazed, she handed a cigarette to Susie who blew

smoke rings, smiled smugly, flicked back her hair.
'It's nothing, I'm not a fucking kid anymore.'

Lara bubbled, 'You're joking, Soos, say you're joking.'
'He's twenty-two, dishy and he drives a white Jag.'

'Susie, you're only twelve. He's too old, whoever he is.'
'Didn't you hear me? He – drives – a – white – Jag.'

'You're too wild, that's your trouble. Pass the fag, meanie.
What's it like then?' / 'Nothing much.' / 'You'll get preggers.'

'He *uses* a Johnny-bag, has loads in case of emergencies.'
'At least he's not stupid. I've never seen a Johnny-bag.'

'I'll get you one, unused, of course, for your sex education.'
'Where did you go, then?' / 'Down a dead end by Avery Hill.

He calls it his Slag Jag. He makes me laugh, my Dan.
He said, I love you very much, Susie. You're ravishing.

C'mon, my turn, and you're supposed to inhale it, like this.'
'It makes me choke.' / 'Lara, you can be so childish. Truly!

Promise not to tell anyone, though.' / 'Course not.'
'There's the boring bell. Here, have a Polo mint.'

HIS HAIRY tentacles grope under a silver lurex halter,
squeeze her bottom, unbutton black satin hipsters,

his fish salivers her mouth as the two protagonists,
under the spotlight of a lonely alley lamp, squirm, gulp

and hum to the grinding of their damp, bony groins.
Slinking off the high street, the alley worms into darkness.

Lara, distracted lookout, lone silhouette, still birdwatcher,
can't blink or breathe, the peepshow reels on bluer.

Daniel unleashes his eel, bags it, thrusts urgently
into Susie's wriggling crotch, as her legs crab his hips,

he humps harder, quicker, until, all gnashing teeth,
he foams off then collapses, a gasping, gnarling grunt.

Not sure whether to applaud or scuttle sidewards,
Lara turns her back. 'Ere, wipe yourself.' He hands Susie

some Kleenex. 'I fancy some chips, d'ya want some?'
'Okay, oh my God. Lara. I forgot.' She goes to call

but he grabs her arm. 'You never said she was a nig-nog.
Don't bring her again. I'll go to the disco alone.

I'm not walking in with that. It's bloody embarrassing.'
Four girls' brogues hurry silently up Eltham's High Street.

Susie feels words swell and subside without surfacing.
Excited at her first disco, Lara, hungry for chat, chirps,

'What's up, Doc? Dan's a real hunk, you know.'

GROOVERS DISCO shimmied with skinny teenagers,
seven abreast, girls in line formation dances: five up,

jump, turn, five back, skip, cross, or singing to
Donny's Osmond's 'And they called it, puppy lu-uu-rr-vve'.

Girls projected their blossomings in skimpy halters
under the beery-eyed lustings of pimply, diffident

ganglys whose flat bottoms stiffly shuffled the walls.
In striped Oxford Bags and check Ben Sherman,

Lara felt pyjama-clad next to the fuck-me cling-ons
of her confidently gyrating peers. She tried to be alluring

but felt as with-it as a teddy bear and sexy as Noddy.
'Why's Daniel ignoring you, Soos?'

'I dunno. He's a pig, actually. I'll ask him. Hold on.'
She marched over to where he stood, arms crossed.

'Why're you ignoring me?' / 'I told you, it's embarrassing.'
'She's not it, she's Lara.' / 'She's a nigger,

a nig-nog, now stick that up your baggy fanny
and chew on it.' Deep crimson, Susie edged back

to her friend. 'What did he say?' / 'Nothing.'
Lara's cheeks burned, looking over she caught his eyes

just as he aped a monkey at her, went 'Hooh! Hooh!'
scratched his armpits, sniggered with his mates.

The room spun, blood sank to her toes, faint, brimming,
Susie's eyes filled too. Both were instantly sapped.

'Let's go home, Soos. I want to go home.'

HOME. I searched but could not find myself.
Not on the screen, billboards, books, magazines
and not in the mirror, my demon, my love
which faded my brownness to a Bardot likeness.

Seasons of youth stirred in my cooking pot,
a spicy mix of marinated cultures, congealed into cold,
disparate lumps, untended, festered.

The grandfather in the hall measured hours, days, months,
a resonant metronome resounding up to my eyrie
where I dragged my brain, a stubborn rhino
into *The Odyssey*, revolutions – Industrial, Agricultural,
French, British royal lines learnt by rote.

Pigeons nested, jabbered, copulated, fluttered off.
Cocooned under sloping ceilings,
my temple of youth, posters of those to die for, escape
from the madding crowd of brothers, deliberately
polluting the Best Room with relentless, noisy farts,
show-time telly, gas fire's hiss.

Escape past the lofty Front Room, unused, jumbled, home
to two broken pianos, a three-legged rocking horse,
moonshone bay windows, up three flights
to the roof where in the silence of the sky, I longed
for an image, a story, to speak me,
describe me, birth me whole.
Living in my skin, I was, but which one?

CHAPTER 13

1974 –

The National Front juggernaut braked in our street,
offloaded two teenage brothers at No 49, swastika

tattoos, shaved heads, crombie coats, Union Jack braces.
Our windows were smashed in soon after, nothing new.

My father spent my childhood chasing those bastards
who'd missiled our windows and skedaddled down the alley.

Daddy grew wings, swooped after them, claws grabbed
dingy collars, hauled to homes, they were deposited

in exchange for formal apologies, financial recompense.
He chased a boy who called for me once, a Trinidadian

in a trilby. He Jessie Owen'd him up Herbert Road
where the boy escaped on a passing 53 bus to Oxford Circus.

I panicked when the skinheads' DMs approached,
crossed the road, and when I saw my father, hid

behind others, turned back, detoured, slid out of view.
It was bloody embarrassing having a black dad.

THOR HEYERDAHL'S book sailed me to Fatu Hiva,
Bora Bora, Raroia, Tahiti. Stony Easter Island

was my destination when I boarded the Woolwich Ferry
on Saturday afternoons for a free ride across turbulent

seas to Silvertown, coconut palms and coral reefs.
I walked around the industrial estates on an expedition

to discover stone adzes, idols, caves full of skulls.
I watched the Thames drift into the South Pacific void

as trade winds guided my balsa raft from the Americas
to the remote Marquesas when I caught the ferry home.

Books enlarged my world. I ate, shat and fucked them.
Words seduced me: xenophobia, melancholia, oscillation,

osmosis, metamorphosis, mulatto, etymology, fellatio.
I stored them in my piggy bank, sought reassurance

from my busy mother, usually marking homework,
for she was now a teacher at Eaglesfield Boy's School

up the road. 'The truth. Am I pretty or not?'
'It's in here that matters,' Ellen tapped against her heart.

'Rubbish,' I exclaimed. 'Am I pretty? Yea or Nay?'
'Look, Lara, your looks come and go but your

personality stays for life. So why not develop that, mnn?'
Crap. It was what you looked like that mattered

and I was repulsive with dark skin and wiry hair.
I vomited up the words *Ugly Bitch* all over my diary

until exhausted, relieved, enraged. I knew myself.

O TO CARTWHEEL knickerless into spring.
I stumbled wobbly on platform clogs, seeking balance.

O to re-birth as a Gauguin lovely, desire, the dilution
of flaky granules in water avec milk ou crème,

subsumed, dissolved, a perfect morning cuppa, ta –
soft sugar, the hard currency of plantations,

brown rocks refined, cane's sugar crystallised
into beautiful white sand, sweet history caught up with me.

Mrs MacDonald. O, she of the Harris tweed, requested
my contralto deliverance of *I Have a Dream* at Assembly.

Me, the only one of out 500 non-frizzy heads. As *if.*
Miss Hughes on a field trip. O, she of the plastic

pearls, a receding ginger bun, ushered me aside,
advised I tone down my dress sense or I'd attract

attention. History determined I should not flaunt
my amazing technicolour Joseph coat and tilting red beret

proclaiming I AM HERE, JE SUIS ICI. Forever.
Toujours. You fucking merdes. I was French noir,

Parisien, peu'aps. How exoteeeeque. I didn't want to
blend in because I couldn't. I wanted to be noticed.

Our planet revolved calmly, patiently, eternally,
sometimes with me, sometimes not.

'DON'T SAY hello then, you miserable lot.'
A loud, nasal mix of churning, crackling globules,

Cousin Beatrice was down from Liverpool for the week,
an Angela Davis wig set off cerise lips, lime green flares

draped over pink suede platforms, at nearly six foot tall
she burst into the Best Room like a gust of wild laughter

arrested mid-flow by the tribe's television spines
supporting crew-cuts, Topsy plaits and wonky Afros.

'Hello Bea,' Juliana managed a quick comma of a smile
as Beatrice nose-dived for Ginevra slouched in the one

armchair near the fire. 'Show some respect, Ginevra.'
She relinquished the throne like a snake, slid to the floor.

'Tell me what happens,' Ladipo whimpered behind a cushion
as Trampas was punched by an outlaw in *The Virginian*.

'Eeeh, but you're a soppy lot,' Beatrice cackled.
'It's only a film, you know.' She flicked open a map-of-Africa

lighter, lit a cigarette, its brown filter made pink and wet.
She curled into the chair like a question mark

as the phone emitted a series of vulgar, jarring burps.
Fabian hurdled the sofa to get it, 'It's for you, Poo-liana.'

Lara shouted out, 'Come and peel the mangoes, Juliana.'
'What's that in aid of?' Beatrice puzzled. 'It's only our joke,'

Lara grinned. 'Mangoes are black food, geddit?'
She shouted out again, the credits rolled, she skipped out

EVENING hit the skyline, diffused the light.
Snapping shortbread in the fading kitchen, Beatrice

awaited Lara, who came in search of custard creams.
'I want a word. What's so funny about being black?'

Lara smirked, 'I'm not black, I'm half-caste, actually.'
'But you're very mistaken, lovey. Ask me how I know?'

Lara tittered, shrugged, went to leave but Beatrice's voice
charged past her, abrasive, abrupt, 'STOP right there.'

Lara exhaled a bored, amplified sigh but sat down,
'I dunno. How d'ya know, Mistress Beatrice?'

'Experience, Lovey, that's how and don't be so cheeky.'
She stubbed out a cigarette, hunched forwards.

'It's time you woke up to the facts or the facts will wake
you up with a slap. The only half you are is half-asleep.

Come up to Toxteth, then you'll know what time of day it is.
We stick together up there, not like you Southerners

with your wishy-washy ways. They don't care whether
your mother's white, green or orange with purple spots.

You're a nigger to them, lovey, or a nigra as I like to say.
Now stick that in your empty shell. Lord knows there's

enough room up there.' Lara yawned, assumed a bland
uninterested expression, studied the wall, intensely.

'YES, you can yawn all right, it suits you.'
Lara's mocking gaze drifted wearily back to Beatrice.

'Look, lovey, I know blacks who were beaten by marauding
whites in the race riots of the Twenties. Marauding, they were.

Do you think they stopped to ask if they were half-caste?
Oh, excuse me, Sir, just before I kick your head in,

is your mother white by any chance?
Those old Africans are dying off now. Mr Ogunsola

went last month, knew my father well, sailed the high seas
together, as chefs. Had a wake, of course, very emotional.

I was hung over for days. It's up to us to carry the mantle,
Lara, don't you see? You with your high-falutin' education.

South Africa? Liverpool is the apartheid state of Great Britain.
Ask me how I know?' / 'How d'ya know, Mrs Mandela?'

'Because I've lived it, that's how. And the young ones
can't get work so they loiter around Granby Street.

Some I've known since they were no more than a glimmer
of lust in their father's eye. They won't give good jobs

to our sort, whether we're plain, milk or even white chocolate,
if you get my drift. Yet we built that great city with our

precious blood. The biggest slave port in England it was...'
Lara leapt up, waved her arms, 'See! Caught you out.

There weren't any slaves in England, Mama Kunta Kinte.'
'Eeeh, you make me sick. Ignorant? Pig ignorant.'

'IF YOUR UNCLE SAM was alive he'd have a story
or two to make your little Afro hair stand on end. Mind,

it's standing on end already, needs a good dollop of grease
and a hot iron comb to straighten out the kinks, and look

at your hands, dry as the Sahara. Of course, your mother
doesn't know any better.' Her voice mellowed, she took

a long, slow puff. 'Lara, lovey, so long as you're of Negroid
stock, diluted or not, you're black. Ask me how I know?'

'How d'ya know, Miss Africa?' / 'The P word, prejudice.
So it's about time you learnt some African ways, eh.

I know the difference between yam and cassava. Do you?
Now, I'll leave it at that. Pop round the corner and get

me some ciggies, and some crisps for yourself. God knows
you can do with some meat on that carcass of yours. And get

a quart of whiskey while you're at it. I'm spitting feathers here.
I might just take you and Laetitia to the flicks tomorrow.

Not that you deserve it. You show no respect whatsoever.
Now, off you go.' As Lara opened the door she mimicked

Beatrice, 'Oh, by the way, you shouldn't smoke, you know.
It gives you bad breath and brown teeth. Ask me how I know?'

'You flippin cheeky little whatsit!' Beatrice flung her empty
cigarette packet at the door, as Lara bounded the stairs whooping.

CHAPTER 14

LAUDATE DOMINUM, Mozart's quavers were brown
cherubims streaming out of the radio in water bubbles,

popping softly against her heart, a soprano's vibrating
breath rose, dipped, haunting. Ellen felt exquisitely sad;

tears seeped quietly, beautifully. The damp kitchen walls
bled, formed rivulets, plaster cracked into maps.

Panes steamed in aged parchment frames, boiling towels
spat and hissed. Two decades of marriage trailed her

like an autumnal country lane, strewn with the withered
debris of summer. Murky puddles were tears of discovery

at births, exasperation at Taiwo's intractability, of loss
as her babies grew, the ecstasy of their love-making –

for in their tenth year they had discovered her orgasm.

Babies? My little ones are nearly adults, my field fallow.
The eldest are leaving soon, in their hearts first, I feel it.
They grow upwards, I grow sideways. I never lost
the excess padding from when they and I were one.

The kettle shrilled, clouds whistled, she rose, languid,
made tea, three sugars today, two next week. Promise.

Deranged Wagner blasted the radio, tenors gargled,
violins sawed, cymbals dustbin-lidded. She turned it off.

Silence or beauty. To have such a choice.
Upstairs her babies watched *Top of the Pops*. Safe.

I STAND for hours, still Madonna lachrymose,
by the religious windows of our chill Front Room,
waiting for one of my children to appear in view;
worry is a damp handkerchief clutched to my breast,
like a fat diva in a tragic opera, I am unconsoled.

My mother worries herself to sainthood most nights,
awaiting one of us to return when we are late, errant
or tempted to run off into adulthood. She fears the briars
of our city's urban jungle, missing persons, Bill Sykes.

My doll's house subsides, my life's work collapses,
would that they stay children forever, my babies.
Barbara Cartland has betrayed me, you see.
I blame myself, I blame Taiwo. You cannot love
by law enforcement, build by bashing foundations.

That's it. No marriage for me. No begetting of sprogs,
dolls to beat when Humpty Dumpty feels bruised.
I despair of my mother's melancholia, my helplessness.
She stands, a Russian doll, peering down the dark street.

My love is a towel soaked in bleach, too long; it tears
away into fragments of myself, then slowly disintegrates.
I see myself in there, waiting, a ghost from this past,
to haunt some future children with my sorry visage.

HIDDEN in the moist entrails of Atlantico,
the basement passage was body-wide, mildewed.

One medieval wooden door arched onto the coal hole,
now populated with a miscellany of saws, shovels,

sinks, enamel potties, antique telephones and lamps
that hung on the stone walls like exhibits in a museum.

To Ellen it was the fridge for birthday jellies and trifles.
Further along was Taiwo's stuffy sanctuary. Shelves

bravely hugged walls, stretch-marked with dog-eared tomes,
newspapers fashioned into skyscrapers spired towards

the wrinkled yellow ceiling until he undertook the ceremony
of burning them in the garden with broken furniture,

branches and a supply of brown-papered sanitary towels.
His trestle-table desk was swollen with household bills,

a tool bag, a rubber plant, a record player. On a concrete
shelf sat a blue and white striped mug holding penny-a-time

black Bic biros, a plastic replica of the Eiffel Tower,
a framed wedding photo and two sullen Yoruba carvings,

his 'n' hers, side by side, grey with dust foundation.
Sometimes, for some perverse reason, Ellen would

venture into this hostile territory, creep round the door,
groan 'Good grief!' and hurriedly exit.

'THERE WAS a child went forth every day.'
Immersed in a slim volume of Walt Whitman, Taiwo

grappled with free verse. He preferred a good rhyme, really,
to chug a poem along. Still, this man took him places.

A tentative tap brought him back. He looked up.
'Yes!' he barked as Lara entered. 'You said you'd tell me

about Nigeria, remember?' / 'Do I look like an imbecile
that I cannot recall what I say? Well, sit down, I will not bite.'

For a change, Lara thought. She squatted on a fresh pile
of newspapers dangerously near the two-bar electric fire.

Taiwo put his back to her, stretched his feet out onto
his desk, said to the window, 'What do you want to know?'

'Everything. Nigeria, your childhood, family, everything.'
He slid his hands around his neck, clasped them,

rocked backwards, closed his eyes. 'Let me see now.
Lagos, she's an island. Sea, river, lakes. Lagos means lagoon,

a Portuguese word but in my language we call it Eko.
They called it The Whiteman's Grave because of malaria.

When it hits the European he knows about it. Ha, ha.
The fish we have there is called electric eel because it

gives you a shock when you hold it.' Lara was getting
impatient. Why was he always so long-winded about things.

'Is your language Nigerian?' / 'Eh! Eh! You really do not
know anything.' Your fault, Lara thought. Your fault.

'MY TRIBE is Yoruba, that is my language.
Then there are the other tribes. The Hausas are illiterate,

the Ibos are cannibals, the Fulanis, beggars, and so forth.
At home we speak Yoruba but at school, English.

In my language names mean something. If you are called
Rotimi you will die young. Just as well I did not give

you that name.' Taiwo chuckled to himself. Lara poked
out her tongue. 'What else do you want to know?'

'What was your mother like?' / 'Oh, very nice.' / 'Yes but
what was she like?' / 'A very nice lady, I can safely say.'

'Well, what was your father like?' / 'He was very nice too.'
This time she rolled her eyes. 'Was he born in Lagos?'

'Oh no, he came from Brazil.' Lara shrieked, 'My grandfather
was Brazilian?' Taiwo cut in, 'Don't shout. Why are you

so excited? You would rather be anything than an African.'
'Tell me about him,' Lara pleaded. Was he very nice too?,

she wanted to add. 'He went to Lagos when he was a boy.
His father brought him, you know, that slavery thing.'

'So we were slaves just like the West Indians?' / 'Never!
We Africans will never be like them. You know they

live in shanty towns with goats sleeping under the bed?
Now that's enough. I have work to do.' She was irritating

him, he decided. He didn't want to go tomb-raiding.
She left, feeling cheated, feeling stirred.

AS LARA approached the terraced box, she chucked
her fag in the gutter, quickly cracked a mint

and buttoned her blouse from chest to neck.
A musical two-tone ding blurred a body in the glassed

hall, it peeped behind the security chain, opened up.
'Hello, hello. Lovely to see you.' They kissed –

one cheek cool satin, the other compact powder puff.
'Let me take your coat.' At four foot ten inches,

with wavy white curls in a 30s bob, Peggy limped
sideways into a flowered room of oak and ornaments.

She fussed in with salads, cold cuts, condiments, cakes
and a china teapot in a Rasta tea cosy. Lara grinned,

glanced over the crew-cut lawn barbered weekly
by one of the tribe for an intoxicating 50p piece.

'Come along, let's eat.' They smiled over the cream
broderie anglaise tablecloth, silver cutlery, engraved

crockery which had been born in the last century.
Lara made a special effort to honour her table manners,

not to slump, scatter crumbs, elbow the table, slouch,
spread too much jam, talk with her mouth full, burp,

say yeh instead of yes or do the unheard of – swear.
They chatted politely but nothing was said.

NO DA COSTA photos memoried the mantelpiece.
Lara noticed. A plain, blonde young man in glasses

saddened the room, her grandfather, Leslie Brinkworth,
who died of lung cancer before Juliana was born.

'So Nana threw herself into loving you children,'
Ellen confided. 'Took her heart off loneliness.'

After an hour Lara fidgeted, tired of censoring
her natural thoughts or doctoring them

before being allowed a sugar-coated exit.
Peggy's script had been written some fifty years earlier,

the stage set then, her home a museum of the 1930s,
the century streamed ahead but she filtered its arrival.

'What's a penis?' she asked Lara, after guiltily
relishing a racy romantic novel Juliana bought her.

Ellen laughed when Lara told her. 'She's always
called it 'down below', you see. Another time

with flickering trepidation and boldness in her eyes,
she ventured quietly, 'A lesbian. What is it, exactly?'

When Lara crossed the portal of No 31 she stepped
out of her personality as if ditching muddy boots,

slipped into the tiny bone bodice of a nineteenth-
century lady, inhaled, and tightly laced up.

'YOUR MOTHER should have married Stephen Brown.
He's a doctor now, has a lovely house in Blackheath.'

History's secrets seeped out when Lara urged Peggy
to recount the good old days, the ones which old ladies

went on about at bus stops, usually while glaring at her.
Not that Peggy ever discussed the split, unpleasantries

were not allowed to sully the air of genteel discourse.
Filling a tray of empty pastry dishes with meat, Ellen

had once revealed, 'Nana sees Auntie Dora often
but she cut me off when I married your father.'

Great Aunt Dora, Lara despised her, and that Jacob
from Germany – how could he be so prejudiced?

Deftly pulling up weeds around the rose bushes, she once
mentioned a burgeoning desire to visit Nigeria.

Peggy twitched, 'What do you want to go there for?
You'll come back looking like a nigger-man, dear.'

Ellen scolded her mother when Lara reported back.
'What have I said wrong?' Peggy protested, knitting,

dropping a stitch, 'She will, if she's not careful.'
'She doesn't mean it,' Ellen reassured Lara, 'It's her age'.

'Not all old people are like that,' said Lara.
'Age has nothing to do with it.'

SUNDAY'S WINTER powdered suburbia with snow,
through the drifts Lara and Peggy trekked west to Mass

in the flurry of chaotic flakes in soundless streets,
houses were iced Christmas cakes lit by fairy-lights.

The taller linked the elder to anchor her limping gait,
in the snow – one penny imprint of a walking stick.

Snow rested on Lara's hair like soap powder.
Liquid, suspended under her nostrils, were dew drops.

She felt loved in this struggling act of shared walking,
though she saw them as she knew others did,

both cameraman and subject of this unusual picture,
the experience was not always an astral one.

They once asked if she was Nana's nurse. Bastards.
When people passed she tensed, anticipating hostility.

Was it her imagination, the disapproving stares? Was it?
They'd called her mother white whore in the Fifties

when she'd courted Daddy, threw insults from cars,
and when the tribe swelled around her in ankle socks.

As they neared St Andrews other journeyers hobbled in,
the organ yawned, nuns in lay gear strummed guitars,

harmonised a folk version of *The Lord's Prayer*.

CHAPTER 15

London, 1980 –

LARA

I BEGAN to dip into my skin like a wet suit,
toes first, warily, wriggled about, then legs all in.

By summer '81 I'd zipped up and dived in head first.
That year I started art school, *Landscape of the Souls*

I called my anarchic blood and black vortices;
I loved exploding the energy of colours, being bold.

Summer heat choked my city's horizon, sluggish clouds
of fumes were mountains of dirt way up in the ether.

Tourists homed in on Piccadilly like brain-damaged fish.
I barged, my large portfolio an aggressive advance guard,

boarded the bus to Camden Town, my squat room,
all purple walls, pampas grass and Mexican mats.

I boogied on down at the 100 Club on Oxford Street,
where pupil-swimming arousal came in the countenance of Josh.

Under his pillar-propping gaze, I tried to dance cool, slyly
studied the Dreads in corners with towels round necks,

trainers, shiny track-suits – red, gold and green striped,
confidently shuffling, moving just off the beat.

Go slower, syncopate, less movement, more weight
We exchanged numbers like French kisses and at 2 A.M.

my creamed knickers rode the night bus home.

JOSH, your limbs were waves. I swam.
Your myriad hands smooth-licked me. The sea.

Flesh. Breath. Flesh. Your tongue swelled in me.
Juiced, me. You, carefully entered, sensing your

way in, alert to my every whimper, responding.
Kiss. Kissed my hips like water, every secreted crevice,

seduced, and only when I cried out first did you go
for the shoot, the spawn game, tadpoles into the pond.

At last, on safe ground, at last, I was, on safe ground.
'Hey, Princess, Let's take the tube train into darkness,'

your public school tones joked, open Ibo vowels
squeezed into nasal tubes, staccato consonants.

Years before I'd made my teenage foray into Brixton,
awed by the tableaux of Atlantic faces, I was

born into whiteness, this was the moon, I was elated.
'Sssss!' The Atlantic Pub, Coldharbour Lane. 'Sssss!

Yuh look nyice, gyal.' Red eyes and Tennent's Extra.
I wore my grandmother's stiff back, her deaf ear.

'Tcha! She favour pork.' I panicked to the station.
With you I merged into Tottenham, the Bush, the Grove,

jostled in markets, pubs under arches, basement clubs.
You squeezed my hand, I was six years old, Daddy?

I poached your easy slope, excited, I was, exalted.
Summer '81 I was touched by the sun.

I WAS JELLY, you were my mould, yet
I could not set, would freeze or throw a wobbly,

criticised your arrogance, your African-at-Eton act.
'You can talk,' you retaliated. 'You're as rootsy

as the driven snow.' You rolled onto me, into me,
my anger drifted downriver like a log.

You loved your skin, polished with cocoa butter,
advised I do the same or I'd 'flake to dust like a relief

on an Egyptian tomb'. You'd coo over my complexion.
'Do you like me or my light-skinned factor?' I said.

'Both, and at least I'm honest before you throw one.
You know I suggest you pursue an academic career.

Paint as a hobby. You have a trunk-full of O's and A's.
I only ever had three choices: law, medicine, finance.

Well, you know how we Nigerians are.' 'Yes', I lied,
then flared up, 'So why are you trying to change me?'

'Because I want to lick your chocolate button nippies.'
You twirled and stroked yourself. I laughed, coalesced.

But felt my summer of passion waning.

'YOU'LL NOT marry a Nigerian if you can't obey me.'
I shook my head slowly. 'You are such a wanker.'

'Ditto, Lara, ditto.' I flung my head back. 'Marriage?
I love the F-word too much, you know...freedom.'

'Just as well, because you don't even know what
Jollof rice is, let alone how to cook it. You're strictly

a fish fingers and mash girl. You'll make a sorry wife.'
He sniffed, smugly sipped his drink, crossed his legs.

'Why don't you put me down, Bertie Wooster,
and who says I only like Nigerian men?'

'It's obvious, you hope some of it will rub off on you.'
'Oh fuck-off, you idiot! Tampon-dick!'

Then he melted, vulnerable in his contrived pose,
the sweet Josh, two years old and thumb-sucking.

I softened, 'Sorry, Josh. Cuddle?' / 'Yes', he pouted,
'A treatie for Wole the Wonder will do the trick.'

I crawled towards him, took his pitiful dejection
in my mouth, chomped, left a shiny, oozing Bounty Bar.

Such a failsafe method of resuscitation.

LAUTREC posters, blue lamps, Portobello pub,
candle-wax bubbles over baroque holders, hedgehog

barmaids have stapled noses, safety-pinned flesh.
I hover in a dungeon alcove, nurse my port, insecure,

wish I'd been born a Holland Park babe, was a funky
half-caste darling, a Cleo Laine jazztress with a voice

that soars, seducing the crowd. My kohl-eyed cohorts
from art school – Hampstead, Chelsea and Fulham,

have tunnelled blow up their nostrils. 'Is that not your Josh?'
Jemima exclaims, glimmering. Hickory, dickory, dock.

Stop. Time clocks. Incongruous in blazer and loafers,
he confidently guides a young Shirley Bassey in sassy

zippy leather to the bar, all kissy-kissy, gooey-gooey, yuk!
I kamikaze my port, emerge bloodened, dazed,

confront him outside. O, to serrate beer bottles.
Scarify his cologned cheeks. Kung Fu his dim sums.

'You like the F-word, remember? We're not wed, Lara.'
My alphabet tumbles, jumbles into a three-year-old's bawl.

'You…you…' I barely whimper, a dissolving aspirin.
Verbals! I need verbals! Please, I want my verbals!

'A hungry gerbil up your hairy arse!' I muster. He snaps,
'Oh do grow up, Lara. Welcome to the real world.'

FURY rode me. A wild buckjumper.
I scalped myself, sacked Josh, speared my nose,

my little Afro ears coiled a C of silver earrings,
I barricaded myself into an army surplus trenchcoat

and fronted a permanent Desperate Dan scowl.
Nuggets of disease erupted on my surface, squidgy

pus-filled hillocks splattered my bathroom mirror.
I denounced my patriarchal father, deconstructed

my childhood, regurgitated appropriated ideas
like closing time vomit. I flirted with Sensi, swooped

on trendy markets for cowries, batiks and sculpture,
I was a walking irradiated automated diatribe, saw

the rapist in every homme, worms in every phallus,
the bigot in all whites, the victim in every black

woman. London was my war zone. I sautéed
my speech with expletives, detonated explosives

under the custard arses of those who dared detour
from my arty political dictates. I divorced my honky

mother, rubbished the globe for its self-destruct sins
and then flung open the Hammer House gates

of my Rocky Horror Hades
and tossed the key.

ABLAZE with the sharp and the syrup, yeh.
I sozzle whisky mixed with Drambuie, neat, just

a tot, a pint, two litres, ta, topped up, topped up;
on brassic days Mr Gordon's Dry Gin, on the rocks,

rocky, slippery, hickory, six bottles Bells
under the sofa, in the sink, in the bin, under the stairs,

a little drop 'ere, a little drop there, droppy droppy
everywhere, now, ready to paint a masterpiece, oops,

mistress-piece, yeh, I mean ten gallons whisky on a drip,
drop, hit the high spot, tick tock, 12 o'clock, havin' a ball,

ready, steady, do a splashy-sploshy 'ere, a splish-splash
whoopshy, ah, the bluesy woes of a sufferin' artist.

Why did you trip me up, Me Easel? Come here now.
Groove on down with Leonard Cohen, hit the floor

with Simone, Bach, a little light Gregorian chanting,
stumble to the loo, prop up, eyes open, keep 'em open,

or the bath'll spin 'n' spin, I feel like, don't wanna feel,
wanna chuck up, eyes shut, in bed, room whirls, upside

down, downside up, wideways in, I weep, I weep, I weep,
I am an old wound, I weep, that has not healed,

        shpin
   shpin   and out.
        shpin

I NIGHTMARE, damply scream into silence...
run backwards into childhood, down Eglinton Road,

his Pinocchio belt pursues, lassoes me; leather belted,
I am legless, my mother in the kitchen is immersed

in the swamp of depression, I skid on her tears –
all the way into the Eighties, Sainsburys, Stepford Wives

checkout, I find a bulging co-star, is he a computer
or just a print out? I sleazily X-ray his Uncle Tom, ding,

dong, *That'll be six pounds and 69 pence, madam.*
I take him home, wardrobe him in leather jock strap,

gun holder, bikers' boots, baby oil his jet buns, play
Black Barbarella to his Kola the Cunt Controller,

he unzips my PVC mini, down the back, black fishnet
stocks, crotch-less satin knicks, red-light thigh-highs, patent,

I pant, trade entrance only, cat o'nine tails, *On yer knees,*
Sweet Jesus! I play second fiddle to his diddle-daddle.

Juice it, Bitch. More. Faster. Faster. You – must – obey.
I won't. I won't. Swoosh. Schwop. Shlick, Tingle

Spread it, take it like a ... I run screaming on moors,
scarecrowed by bibles in batted capes, coarse

cloth and clog villagers, I am stoned into rivers...a car
alarm goes off, I awake, relieved, moist, dehydrated.

Say ten Hail Marys, my child. Yes, Father.

'YOU'RE AN UNDRESSED genius, Lara.' Trish unwraps
my magnum opus on the floor of our latest makeshift

gallery, another empty shop in Marylebone High Street.
I laugh, proud of my painting, a life-sized bottle, my naked

self going glug glug to the bottom. 'It's called Booze,' I say.
'Eat yer art out Jean Michel-Basket. This is London-stylee.

My influences are Hackney, Afro-beat and Blue Peter.'
I stand back, watch Trish contrast the freshly-white walls.

'Never was the Nefertiti from Neasden so beautiful,'
I declare grandiloquently. ''Tis indeed true,' she grins,

'Many have commented on my timeless, regal beauty.'
She spins the floor like a Whirling Dervish, ululating.

'I'm going away,' I call out. / 'Yeh, yeh, another fancy.'
'No, for real this time. I'm hitting the road, Jack, Trish.

I've had it. Ain't no Saatchi gonna doubloon my satchel.
I've hoarded some coppers in my piggy. It'll last a while.'

Trish stopped, stared me out. 'It's just escapism, Lara.
We're best friends. Don't bugger off now, you old cow.'

'I s'pose I am escaping. I'll soon know if it's from myself.
Come with me, live a little, leave this cage. Anyway,

when this show comes down, it's toodle-oo from me.
I'm going to trundle my way across Europe.'

IT'S PISSING DOWN out the jeep, out the door, pissoir,
perched for a pee, cloth over knees, mobile loo,

out of view, 'cept for spyin' lorries who honk
and perv and rev on down the slick autobahn – wet wipes,

towels, maps, Stanley knife, icebox, cassettes, the long
and winding, yellow brick, to follow, wherever I lay my

home, hat, the road, we spiral around, gorge on satay chips,
salami, Belgian chocs, sauerkraut, Austrian beer, vin,

brie slabs in French sticks, olives, artichokes, a million
pastas, dip doughnuts in cups of hot, thick chocolate,

we brawl, sulk, make up, Trish and I, hold our breaths
as borders fly into blurs, our old Volkswagen Beetle

pipped by sleek Mercs, and on down Spain's dry African
spine, we overheat, slow down, rest, renew, stagger

farting up the Costas, ex-pat colonies, retired colonels,
fish 'n' chips, Brit bars, we flee, exhilarate, compass the sun,

tunnel the mountainous Med, zipped nights on sand,
Brindisi, Patras, Piraeus, Heraklion, Rhodes, Marmaris,

we edge, we ease, we secure ourselves onto ferries,
chug, we sail the clean Aegean east.

EMPTY ROADS guzzle us up, frazzled tarmac,
smoking horizons, lunar mountains, ploughed land, we
snipe, bicker, sweat, as we fizz east, yavas yavas
slowly, slowly, shallow breathing, fantasting baths
of iced water, dream of a full Sunday roast, all of a sudden:
spuds, cabbage, gravy, salivate, PG Tips, in the heat,
fried breakfast? ketchup, even. We become more British,
Trish and I, darker with the Turkish sun, yet less
aware of race for we are simply: İngiltere.
Our tracks lead to dusty villages, musty beds, my brain
contains three thoughts only – petrol, food, shower.
London retreats, a dislocated memory, immaterial now.

Finally,
        I flop on an old hippy beach for a year
                                    and stop.
Under the Asian sun my armour roasts, rusts,
falls off in bits,
is swept out by the tide.   I watch it bob off,
                                    new
flotsam,
study the twinkle twinkles in the firmament at night,
go for a midnight dip,
                and emerge,
                            the sum of all my parts.

HE SMELT of the sea. Hakan. And fish –
during the day. Bedtime of Imperial Leather Soap
and at midnight our bodies made love.

A fisherman, he stitched nets, the far side of the beach.
I watched his back, stripped, hairless, brown, broad
from rowing boats.
                    I left my tent early morning,
swam over, tiny fish slipping down my costume.

He poured thick coffee, outside his cabin, summers
near the sea, he said, winters in his mountain village.

Hakan. Tatar-man, sharks flecked in his narrow eyes.

Some nights he rowed me out to sea, *Mehmet II*,
a larger boat, awaited, and nets spread for a wide catch.
I lay on deck, cushioned against salted wood, waves
licked, caressed, the moon, lolling of the sea. Perfect.
I was whole. Closed my eyes, tried to picture my real
life but only sky appeared. He worked silently, oblivious.

I was seasonal, perhaps. It was safe to love Hakan,
both knowing I would not stay forever.

        For a while I was a fisherman's moll,
by the sea, on beaches, on the fallen stone plinths of ruins,
in a cabin, the woods, by the Med.

                            And when I left,
Hakan did not look up from mending his nets.

CHAPTER 16

1987 –

ELLEN

I WAS her daughter for fifty-four years,
shall be keeper of her grave now, next to Father's.

Eighty-two years, two wars of this world, in pain
towards the end, she surmounted all trials, a fortitude

I inherited, raising my eight brown-skinned children.
I held her through the night, my mother, my child,

last air gasped out. I held her as she held me when
I cried my first breath. Snow fell all week, freezing

our old away, taking my mother away. Snow fell, painting
Swiss pictures, pretty sights for the dying, no burial

for the dead. Bless you, my mother, for your teachings,
your prayers, your caring, our friendship in later years.

Bless you, my mother, for the love you lived for each
of your grandchildren, through all your disapproval.

You weakened, I cradled, knowing you were passing,
my mother, my constant, I cuddled you with a love

that will not weaken with time. Ice morning this.
Bracken coated, stark out the window. Your face grey.

Slate grey. Thing, grey. Rock grey. Empty. Earth grey.
You were gone, and I cannot, I cannot, stop crying.

Snow turns to sludge. Spring will come.

CHAPTER 16

DRIZZLE. Reluctant Wednesday. Smoker's sky.
Assortment of cars pull in. The da Costas emerge

for the funeral of Mrs Peggy Brinkworth, *née* 1905.
Cenotaph brothers, square-jawed, square-shouldered,

as if scanned off the pages of *Ebony* magazine,
four sisters lower their hats to conceal puffy eyes.

Lara watches two shadows arrive; 'faces of the unlived,'
she observes – Dora and Jacob grip Ellen's hand

in a long lost gesture and Ellen forgives with a smile.
Dora proffers Lara a limp hand, 'Lovely to meet you.'

Lara stretches her lips over teeth, wants to say,
'You're behaving like the Queen Mother doing the rounds

with the disadvantaged.' Taiwo plasters on a wide
Black and White minstrels' beam, then rips it off when

they move inside. Dora's offspring confide to Ellen
that it was because of the war, the Jewish factor,

their parents wanted to fit into suburbia like red bricks,
crazy-paving relations would have made them stand out.

Inside the loveless Chapel of Death, Lara mouths hymns,
afraid of the choke that will sound if she sings.

LARA

WHEN NANA DIED the sea began to surge,
rushed into my ears at night, a conch shell,

played in different octaves, music, vague lyrics,
words formed by waves and wind, whooshing.

Iyabo was born a year later, to Juliana.
'Mother Returns', named by my father, identikit

of Nana, who would surely have idolised her
hazel eyes, thin nose, blonde hair, ivory skin.

The sea would not leave me, though, its warm
waters enveloped me; I felt buoyant, floating.

One morning I awoke, not sure if I'd slept at all,
the sun was a Tibetan monk-orange falling onto

the cascade of red-tiled houses down Camden Road –
sunrise at sea. Someone materialised in my room,

like photographic paper in developer, an image formed,
a woman, I thought, dark-skinned, tall, then

she faded out into nothingness, only air and atmosphere,
but the music, the wind, the tune encircled me.

'Bring him home,' it sang, 'Bring him home'

CHAPTER 17

LARA descended fearfully over desert into Lagos,
her garrulous co-passenger full steam: 'She vomited

sticks, snakes and turtles. Yes! One lady was pregnant
five years, her baby born with long hair and teeth.

Be careful. We have X-ray eyes here.'
The customs officer eyed the da Costa trio greedily.

'Welcome!' He examined their bags. 'You have a gift for me?'
Yellow taxis queued patiently in the soupy heat

but their owners charged the arrivants like players
in a rugby scrum, 'Taxi! Taxi! Come with me – O!'

'Ah! My people!' Taiwo exclaimed as their driver
revved out of Murtala Muhammad Airport towards

the island city that had been a memory for so long.
Bumper to bumper, crusty bone-shakers emitted

clouds of billowy black particles; at midnight the city
boiled over with crowds, beggars negotiating

the alleys between cars, thrusting handless arms
through windows; miles of candle-lit women lined

streets, crouched behind wares, coils of dried fish,
peanut cones, orange pyramids, hessian bales of rice.

Taiwo had not been back in forty-four years, yet
this was the place he called home.

SLICED DODO browned, crisped in hot oil pans,
were wrapped, sold for a few naira on the streets;

butchered meat salivated on stalls, bleeding pink flesh
exposed, was skewered, to drip fat over flames;

herons elegantly plundered smoking refuse tips
like mobile daffodils; storm drains festered pungently;

Fuji pounded out of door-size speakers, rattling
the ribs of those passing, vibrating through soles.

'Yaba! Yaba! Yaba! – Yaba! Yaba! Yaba!' – clanking
jalopies hurtled past, men hanging off the sides;

'Oyinbo!' children shouted after Lara. 'It means
whitey,' Taiwo told her. Women wearing gelé,

buba, iro made her circumnavigate them, some
with bleached faces – burnt and discoloured;

arguments erupted like a volley of attention-seeking
bullets, street theatre improvised; people eyeballed Lara,

a coach passed, all heads about-turned to stare.
She inhaled the thick, spiced aromatic air of Lagos,

drunk in its vitality, absorbed the muggy heat.
This is the land of my father, she thought.

I wonder if I could belong.

Central Lagos. December '93. Sweltering.
From Tafawa Balewa Square jaunts the ageing Nigerian,

tripping over his mind, curls painted black, a camera
worn from his neck is a trophy or gold medallion, after all

he is a 'been-to'. Down Catholic Mission Street –
England-lady, plumpie, short, pale-streaked hair like grass.

Into Ibosere Road, Lara follows – tall, modern Afro-mix,
young, designer-brown, Levis, T-shirt, trainers.

The old Brazilian Quarter on Lagos Island, at last,
the 'where?' – not known by name anymore.

They walk, stop for minerals: Fanta, Coke, pass
new bungalows, invisible ghosts, chickens dart the road.

A strange fire ignites Taiwo, children's faces,
he searches them for his own. Wind stirs up the dust.

He must find his childhood house, it is urgent, suddenly.
How his town has disillusioned him – skyscrapers,

squandering, polluted lungs of squalor, too many flies
have dimmed its light. It is crazy. Suddenly he wants

to whoop, cartwheel, spin the air. Instead he freezes.
There, next to the Elf petrol station, is No 18 Ibosere Road.

His castle of childhood, of love, of memories. Home.
The past swamps him like a drowning man.

DAZZLING. Whitewashed. He leans on the balcony,
a new short-sleeved shirt, grasshopper green,

beige slacks, squeaky brown sandals, polished skin.
His forehead is damp, jaw papaya soft, he bares

a regiment of brilliant white teeth though it wasn't
fashionable to smile in photographs of the day.

He puffs his chest. He is a man. Seventeen.
Soon he is off to a country called Euphoria.

The woman looking down into the box camera
is in her adiré best, is damming her tears.

All she can see is her little boy Taiwo, five,
with a lovely dimple and a love of dumplings.

1993

Fast forward. The man. The balcony. Cracked.
Cars zoom past, noisy as a washing machine's last spin.

Skin clings to bones where once it sheltered them.
Shoulders hunched with a lifetime's tension, somewhere

around his knees, his age shows. Juicy lips dried out.
The young woman, his daughter, taking photos

with her brand new Olympus sees through her father
to the boy. Hopeful. Before he ate the bitter kola nut.

He has revealed himself. Here, his childhood home.
His jaw fossilised, with the gritting of it.

'DEAD BODIES in the streets for days, open sewers,
ambushes on the road. I heard it all over the years.

To be honest, I was frightened.' Ellen looks over
as boisterous girls with blue dresses and dusty legs

scoot past the hotel patio. She squints at the sun sneaking
up over unfinished roofs, dreading its sticky lethargy.

She sips tea, grimaces at the condensed milk inside.
A gecko hovers on the ceiling; she tightens her wrapper,

moves her chair away. 'The people here are so warm.
We English are such cold fish, I realise that now.'

Lara is doing Yoga exercises: Tree Pose, Mountain Pose.
Two dogs, wretched as ancient teddy bears, scuttle past.

Ellen perks up 'The only thing that bothers me
are the mosquitoes, to be honest. Maybe I'll finish

my teaching career here. They're hungry to learn,
not like those ungrateful terrors back in London.'

Lara stops stretching. 'You're a few decades late, Mum.
I'm pretty sure they want African teachers now.'

Ellen puts down her mug, 'I expect you're right.'
She keeps one eye on the sun clearing the mosque.

Lara assumes Warrior One Pose, then Warrior Two.
'What I'd give for a cappuccino and croissant right now,'

she says before going into Upward Facing Dog.
Ellen giggles, gets up as the sun hits her, moves inside,

walking like an oyinbo in an African wrapper.
'You must adjust, dear. Adjust.'

HENRIQUE OLIVEIRA'S cottage is dead.
Boarded up, crossed planks, termites. Taiwo exclaims

melodramatically, 'It is the cankerworm of neglect!'
He pontificates as if on a milk crate at Speaker's Corner,

haunts the Quarter like a refrain, trying to kiss-of-life
his barefoot boyhood, his age of innocence.

The Quarter fans out from the GPO to the YWCA
in Broad Street, roads sweep up in hills to the left.

Taiwo's classmates inhabit houses which Brazilian ancestors
built when they returned over a hundred years ago.

They guzzle Nigerian beer on doorsteps, eat Kola nuts,
eulogise the halcyon past, bemoan the here and now.

Lara walks with Taiwo, vigilant, reprimanding him
for flashing wads of naira or hailing taxis in the dark, drunk.

He boasts to his cronies that he has two women to boss
around in Lagos, until her eyes shoot darts of ice

at him, decades of frozen anger, and his words quake
mid-sentence, stream back into his mouth.

On her last day in Lagos she surveys the Atlantic
from fashionable Bar Beach on Victoria Island

where the ocean attacks the sand in hostile waves.
Her bare feet sink deeper as each wave retreats

and she toys with the idea of crossing over to Brazil,
completing her own three-point turn.

CHAPTER 18

Lagos Island, Nigeria, 1931 –

LAGOS ISLAND cooking. It simmers all day long
till twilight creeps in and the sun slips into another time zone.

Here sun is omnipotent: a scorched orb blazing a lazy
blue sky, everyone and everything bakes. It pounds down

onto the white-washed houses of the Brazilian Quarter,
steam rises from the swamps of Five Cowrie Creek

named after the old ferry fare of cream-curled shells
to Victoria Island. But those were the old days, today

they use the nickel penny and paper pound for in 1861
the island was stolen by the British. Now they own it.

This is a sizzling, buzzing island with long, long streets,
some wide or winding, others climbing, others cramped

where the Agudas live. They've been back a long time.
Shades style skins, stories colour sins: burnt almond,

caramel, umber, ivory, rust – antiquities now, long dark
wheals form striped designs across some backs, others

have the stamp of ownership burnt into baby flesh.
All were marked for life. Ships sailing sugar canes,

slave legacy surnames: Salvador, Cardoso, Roberto,
Evaristo, da Souza, da Silva and da Costa.

NO WIND. No air. Red-necked lizards crawl up walls.
Dogs lie in the shade of the sprawling branches

of mango trees – slumped, clammy, panting.
Thirsty foliage, dust-flaky-dry, aches for the sweet

voluminous wet of the rainy season. Fishing boats
sit motionless on the beach, coarse, weather-beaten

sails hang limply from rusty masts. Lethargy claims
Lagos like a slothful buffalo wading through mud.

In Ibosere Road, the majestic Zenobia stands,
a wooden statue on her veranda, sweats droplets

and surveys: palm-thatched huts for the latest arrivals,
flamboyant sobrados for wealthy Agudas, with balconies,

balustrades, tiled roofs, arched doorways and windows.
Senhor da Rocha of the Water House in Kakawa Street

nods to her as he purrs slowly by in the back of his new
Model T Ford Coupé. A crowned crane, owned by Dr Maja,

struts pompously down the centre of the road – ignored.
Vincento Ferriera lurches around a corner, palm wine

slurping in two calabashes from his wonky bicycle.
Next door the ample Yinka sways to market, maid in tow.

And Zenobia – wife, iya, solitary, lovely as a flame tree,
the rattle of words in her head as intrusive as crickets.

FAR FROM her Sowemima family in Abeokuta, Zenobia
showered in the holy water of the Irish nuns in Nigeria.

Thus was she plucked from the ordered convent garden
of these wan brides of Christ by Gregorio, treble her years

and desirous of a madonna negra to reproduce himself.
'Why, of why, must I be chosen but cannot choose?' she cried.

'The answer, a fine dowry, so I could be wed. Kind enough
I hoped to love him but at night I yearned to be held, to feel

the pleasure of my husband's warmth. He turned his back
and the moon, watching, threw light on his snoring body.

I could barely breathe, my waters broke, I birthed twins:
Taiwo tasted the world first, Kehinde brought up the rear.

This was love, none could match it; all day they slept
tied with a wrapper, breathed hot air into my back,

life into me. But nights were restless, my dreams took me
to Abeokuta, home of gentle hills, and Olumorro,

the rock overlooking the town, its caves large enough
to hide children from slave-catchers. The Guardians,

two women who lived in the rock, one my grandmother.
Her daughter strapped me to her back. How I miss

my mother, it grows with my young married years.
When the sun rises over the lagoon, filters our room orange,

I gather my crying newborns into my arms and for the hours
between sun-up and down, give them all the love I crave.'

THE TWINS grow into podgy little puddings
with a gleaming cropped head of black curls apiece.

Taiwo's huge, bush-baby eyes are mischief-makers,
his scuffed knees knock together when he walks

and he dips fat fingers into egusi stew when Mama's
not looking, darts lizard-speed out the door when she does

and on down the road, dodging the whacks of irate elders.
He drags Kehinde along to the cemetery, out of bounds,

high and full of mango trees, ripe with bursting fruit.
But he wants bats, hanging from branches, upside down,

wings closed, nocturnal, somnolent – bats – he shoots
them down with his home-made catapult, splits one open,

roasts it over a fire, feels like he's a grown-up, throws one
at Kehinde to scare her and she screams the mangoes down.

When blood rushes from her hand like a headless chicken,
Taiwo knows he's dead already. He picks up a large stone,

bashes the culprit until it's all blood and dark mush,
then tries to carry Kehinde home like he's a hero

carrying the war wounded. But inside his legs
are all jellyfish wobble and his eyes the sea at high tide.

KEHINDE will die young, like a butterfly.
She was born with a caul draped over her body.

Talibi! they said, *Talibi!* so she can see the future
but she will never see herself in her dreams.

For now all she has to do is bat her baby eyes
and watch the anger of adults dissolve into air.

Kehinde? No. It must be that rascal boy Taiwo.
Her mama takes her to the African General Hospital

where the doctor gives her bandages, biscuits
and tells her she's the sweetest little girl.

She wears a look of brave sorrow as she proceeds
back down Ibosere Road swamped by fussing adults

and flanked by a gaggle of excited children
who skip ahead announcing her triumphant return.

When Taiwo, cowering on the steps, looks for sympathy,
Kehinde sneakily pokes out her tongue, before she's swept

inside with all the ceremony of an ancient African court –
by a grim-looking mama to whom Taiwo is now invisible.

She is the tragic Yoruba princess for the afternoon,
pampered, petted, and right now stuffing her mouth

with glistening, freshly-cooked, corncakes.

GREGORIO, a face serene as a Benin bronze,
wears a Homburg tilted oh so, moves from the hips,

his shoulders follow. His slow, measured step
says he knows he's somebody. Taiwo knows

he's God for when he enters the road he sees
people move like the parting of the Dead Sea.

His daddy's so tall his eyes can spot Taiwo
quivering like a maimed bird a mile away.

His daddy can see through wood, stone and bone.
He has houses, servants and suits so sharp

you can draw margins with the trouser crease.
When he towers above his son, an elephant at night,

Taiwo feels like a fly about to be stepped on.
His twins bow when he enters, speak when

spoken to, do not look him in the eyes and do not,
I repeat, do not, play games in the cemetery.

When Gregorio demands answers,
Taiwo's voice dries up like the water pump

from Scotland at the end of the street which splutters
but delivers nothing. When his daddy beckons

him to follow, he feels like the bat, all mashed up inside.
The rest of the world ceases to exist for Taiwo.

There is just him and his daddy containing an anger
as deadly as the sharks beyond the reef.

WHITE SQUARE ROOM, plastered walls, curtains drawn
to keep out the pervasive sun and flies. Stern,

high-backed chairs, elaborate gilt-edged cabinets
made by Aguda craftsmen. Spotless wooden floor bearing

no sign of this home's inhabitants. God and his family
in painting, ornament, cross – adorn walls. Gaslight

shadows the room yellow; a rocking chair, squeaking.
Gregorio – legs astride, stone eyes, lips dry, tirade

running on like a waterfall. 'You, boy, are as worthless
as the rotting fish on the beach. Your brains are smaller

than a tsetse fly. You have the manners of a hog,
the discipline of a mad bush-boy. Ah! Are you my son?'

Taiwo stood to attention like a toy colonial soldier,
tears crusting his plump cheeks. This was the easy part.

After came ten licks, a worn leather belt kept hanging
on the door for this purpose. His mama entered,

served Gregorio with jollof rice, chicken, moi-moi,
while Taiwo put his right finger on the ground,

raised his left leg behind him in a straight line, and stayed
motionless. His head throbbed, nose burned, ran

with water, legs shook, groin split in two. Just before
he collapsed, his daddy wiped his mouth with a napkin,

cleared his throat, said, 'May that be a lesson to you.'
Zenobia took him to bed, but before he heard her say

'I love you but you must behave yourself,' he was asleep.

CRUEL HARMATTANS conquered the south, sweeping
down from the Hausa desert, each grain of sand a scorpion,

whipping dust into spiral storms of hot air, dry heat,
thick with swirling particles; the city turned in on itself,

shut door, shuttered window, until the rains came,
swelling crumbling soil. And the boy grew

into the hard green fruit of the slim paw paw tree.
And when the sun graced this island which pulled

people to its shores like bees to a honeycomb,
Taiwo dreamt of exploring the worlds these migrants

left to memory: Lebanon, Libya, China, Syria, India,
Ghana, Sierra Leone, Gambia, Europe.

He took his sandaled youth to Apapa Docks, watched
the émigrés disembark from the huge cargo ships

that streamed into port, horns resounding for miles.
He taunted the 'sailor's children', pale, raggedy products

of prostitute and European who lived on the streets.
If he wandered too near the axis of port life, policemen

in pith helmets, khaki shorts, long woollen socks, shooed
him away. Taiwo took off, skinny legs at a canter,

travelled across his island from port to lagoon to swamp.
He luxuriated in the warmth of his sunlit home, as if a voice

deep, olden or from his future tense was telling him
to remember, enjoy, childhood would not last forever.

TAIWO

I AM A BOY, I go like fire, why walk when you can run?
Watch me race past Mama Lopes in Tinubu Square,

at her stool frying akara bean cakes for over fifty years,
my mouth waters as I whiff past. I hear the organist

in the cathedral then the muezzin in Shitta Mosque, dodge
kids playing hockey with rams' horns on sticks, girls

playing the skipping-clapping game of Oya, and old men
playing Ayo under a guava tree. In Carrena Street I catch

the leering, firefly eyes of Ma Amponsah as her slurred
voice suggests I partake of her gin: I leap across the road,

collide with the sanitary inspector in his creased grey suit,
'Pardon, Sir,' I say into my chin and, when I look up,

Laurenço Nobre, the dog-catcher, stands before me
carrying a noose threaded through a bamboo pole.

I head off down Catholic Mission Street where Ahmed,
a boy with no legs, whizzes by on his wooden trolley

on wooden wheels, I race whippet-fast past musicians playing
Omolé and on to the Race Course where we celebrate

Empire Day, dash down to the Marina, avoiding the wrath
of Mr Pickering outside his store. (He calls us picanninies,

we call him 'dog-lips' before scarpering.) At the beach
I see older cousin Sam among the palm trees and canoes;

we will catch conger eels but I feel a breeze against
my cheek, and suddenly remember, I have a visit to make.

My grandfather Baba Aguda is a long time waiting for me.
I freeze mid-motion, turn on my heels, and run...

SEA-BLACK, wave-curved lips and decayed yellow
teeth parted to release a guttural, rum-rich laugh,

when Taiwo, the panting long-legged boy, flung
himself on the wooden veranda in respectful greeting

of his grandfather, who spat out the pulp
of his frayed chewing stick, flicked back the sleeves

of his bright blue agbada and called gently.
'Come, come,' he said and with an oba's sweep of his arm,

drew the fear-drenched child to his chest.
'You think I would hurt you? You are my bones.

I would not hurt myself, would I? Eh heh!
So the octopus has finally tied up your tongue. Yes!'

'No, Sir, but I was running so fast I forgot.'
His Baba, more grand, more imposing than any chief.

Oh to run his fingers over the rivulets on his face,
to count the white coils crowning his head.

Baba's sackcloth cheek scraped Taiwo's soft new skin.
He felt the vibrations of his grandfather's bass voice

resonate through skin, bones, down to his tingling toes.
'Now go sit on the floor, don't fidget, shut up

and listen as if you are a bat with no eyes.'

CHAPTER 19

Pernambuco, Brazil, 1840 –

BABA

THE GODS born me on a fazenda in the hills of Brazil.
(Baba's sonorous rasp of cigarillos and cachaças deepened

his jaded brown eyes glazed, affixed this memory place.)
Born into the time of slavery, ten long decades ago.

Yes, your Baba came into this world a chattel, owned
by Senhor Fernandés da Costa, sugar plantation owner.

I Leonardo, came out behind my twin brother Gilberto,
sons for Antonio and Severina, my mãe and my pai.

Mãe cut cane with me strapped to her back.
Palm tree tall, she had heavy breasts, I can still recall

her hard muscles moving against my squashy little body
and the rhythm of her steady *Shwop! Shwop! Shwop!*

When I was able to run and carry, I worked the fields.
My muscles forever ached like the fever, exhaustion

made my walk an old man's drag, my stomach gnawed itself
and always the shadow of fear, the long-haired men

mounted on silent stallions silhouetted against the sun.
No link to the outside world, cut off in time, losing time,

I felt my whole lifetime would be spent killing sugar cane.
My scrawny back arched like a sickle.

CHILDREN FORGET what is too painful to remember.
For years I could not imagine Mãe's face or form or voice.

One night she was a husky lullaby soothing us to sleep,
the next, stirring in morning's ghostly light, she had vanished.

Mãe had been the river I swam in. The river held me,
kept me buoyant. I trusted river. When Mãe left

I cried the free-flowing tears words cannot reason away,
felt the seed of Rage root itself and try to murder me.

Nights, Mãe had cradled Pai, an infant in her arms,
now I cuddled Gilberto to sleep like he was my child,

rocked him when nightmares snake-attacked him awake
in the darkness of our hot wattle and daub hut.

But when we boys exploded in fury, Gilberto was worse.
Pai threw cold river water over us, tried to drown Rage.

'Calm down, my sons. If you lose your
temper you will come under the lash of the overseer.'

We are slaves. We must control our feelings. Always.'
My anger went underground, where it smouldered.

TEN BLISTERED SUMMERS raised me on that remote fazenda
as boyhood dissolved into a blur of sugar cane fields.

Without rites of passage we were the forgotten people,
sweating our laboured days till darkness made us blind.

Sundays – a time of rest, to ease our knotted muscles,
fortify our hearts, while we prayed for eternal salvation.

Me and Gilberto gazed the same reflection in the river,
grew quickly like reeds, ripples on our hard stomachs.

The gods chiselled our cheekbones into bowls.
Fine. We were fine, and noticed, were sent to serve

the old Senhor in his great stone house beyond the fields.
A sweeping staircase spiralled to a domed ceiling

of heavenly, stained-glass angels; oil paintings of porcelain-
skinned noblewomen travelled the length of the walls;

golden tapestries of flaming red dragons hung in alcoves;
there were chandeliers, chests of lace, chairs with lion's legs,

stuffed alligators and jaguars, cupboards of bone china,
rugs of the Orient and a floor of polished mahogany.

We were put in purple livery and ordered to sleep outside
Senhor's room so he could summon us in the night.

LIKE A SUN-DRIED tobacco leaf, prematurely aged,
our pai withered. We heard about quilombos,

escapees in the hills, who lived together, fought
bandeirantes with bow and arrow. We boys so longed

to join them but Pai told us No. Sundays,
me and Gilberto would sit by the river and hear

Pai's stories passed on by his mother Calixta,
once a free woman named Abimbola in Yorubaland.

He spoke: '*Before this slavery-time there was a lady
in the old country who bore fifteen children*

*and lived to a great age. Wizened, wiry, wise,
her face a map of creases, and when she gripped you,*

*they said, you could feel the pulse of blood pumping
through her veins like a river rushing on.*

*She was my mystical memory grandmother
and she spoke from the deepest part of she-she-self,*

*and everyone was hypnotised by the drum-drum rhythm
in her voice as she spoke the lives, loves, losses*

*of our people. There, by the lapping waves, spitting fire
cackling on, flickering shadows onto she old-old face.*'

My pai told me this story with such tenderness
as if he had been there, but it was only a story passing on.

Pai should have sat at her feet as a free Yoruba boy.
Instead he was a no-man who never sailed home.

WHEN AFRICANS came from the coast, I dreamt the ocean.
It was vast, empty, man could see through time.

I saw Pai evaporate in the feverish swamp of malaria,
his waterlogged flesh steamed, lips drooled yellow sap.

One humid night Pai crossed over into the blue of dawn,
I planted the seed of a baobab tree over his buried body,

watched it grasp at life over years that gave me manhood,
resolved to one day plant a tree from Pai's bone-fed seed

in Yorubaland, his home across the ocean – and ours.
When we were grown into men, Senhor Fernandés died,

Before death his sunken eyes were desperate.
His favourite act had been to order a public flogging,

put melted wax on his victim's lacerated back
and make us watch as he slowly peeled it off.

In his will he bequeathed we brothers our freedom.
We celebrated by ripping down his youthful portrait

from above the fireplace in the banqueting hall,
taking it to the river, smudging shit over it then watching

it burn as the fire threw an eerie light onto our faces.
From the loathing distorting Gilberto's features,

I knew then that Rage would consume him.

BABA

WE WERE EMANCIPADOS, with papers to prove it.
Like war-torn soldiers we trekked from moon to moon

through the wilderness of Bahia to the city of Salvador,
where, perched like gulls on a windswept cliff,

the ocean gave me breath when I first saw and loved it.
We slept on the beach between cactus and bush, watched

Bahianas balance baskets of fish on wrapped heads,
brightly-layered skirts flounced by revolving hips,

long thin pipes gripped by teeth in hardened mouths.
We were seduced into the bosom of Salvador's bustling

streets: Terreiro de Jesus, Cidade Alta, Largo do Pelhourino.
Ah, Salvador took us all – Africanos livres and escravos,

the brancos who battered the cobbles in jangling carriages,
the sararas, morenos, mulattos, who did not see us

as we scavenged for food or begged for work at the docks.
In time we hulked great containers of sewage about the city,

slept on mats in a passage in the back streets of Pelhourinho,
gulped the sweet fire of cachaça in bars past darkness,

where Gilberto fired his pain in blood and body battles
and I'd slip to the shore with a free serving girl, Joana,

its plump beach spread to take the plunging, frothing waves.
Then the current suddenly dragged me fathoms under

Gilberto was knifed to death by sailors at the docks.
We had survived twenty-two summers as one.

I TOOK OFF for the jungle where I could lose myself.
My beloved Gilberto had fitted me like a second skin.

Now I felt skinless, my nerves raw, exposed, weeping.
Terrorised, I shook as I fought the terrible urge

to slash my wrists and float face-down in the river.
Instead I ripped my flesh with clawed fingernails,

howled under the moon or huddled under like a crab.
I stayed in the jungle until I could contain myself.

When I returned I was a changed and lonesome man.
I badgered Paulo, the mulatto son of a coffee merchant

to teach me writing and reading. I taught what I learnt
at midnight in a candlelit cave while Salvador slept.

One of my pupils, Arsenio, introduced me to Capoeira
the ancient fighting dance from the old country.

At last I could let Rage out. I whirled, dodged, leapt,
did back-flips, headstands, handless cartwheels,

sweat sprayed out of my body like jets in a fountain,
I became a running stream as the berimbau's pounding

beat sent shock waves through my thrashing limbs.
You should have seen me then, Taiwo. So lithe, so graceful,

filled with the passion of one who is blessed with life.
Salvador, city of loss, had become my place of hope.

'CANDOMBLE has always been in my blood.'
Agostinho spoke in a thin, high-pitched voice, bald head

stooped so that his back nearly formed a half-moon;
so tiny he merged into a corner of his workshop,

stacked ceiling-high with dark bolts of material.
'I have coffee, want some?' I sat down, mesmerised.

Was he expecting me? He was expecting me.
I needed trousers. Agostinho, the tailor, was cheapest.

'In Bahia Candomblé has been a secret for centuries.
You are ready to know it.' / 'But I am Católico,'

I said, feeling my strength drain away as I spoke.
'Of course. They captured our bodies and our spirits also.

On the fazendas it was washed out very early on
but I am a babalao. I will teach you about Oxala,

Osumare, Ogun, Eleggua, Egun, Xango – Cabo Sile!
Yemanja, Goddess of the Sea – she is your special orixa.'

Then his voice dropped, a broken, croaking sound,
'You knew your mother but not for long. She sends word

that she watches over you. Light a candle, pray to her.
Do not worry, your father and brother are at peace.'

'But where does it all come from?' I asked.
'From the orixas, from the ancestors. Your trousers

will be a perfect fit. Come in two weeks. Now go.'

MY SON SWAM into this world, cooked in Joana's juices,
roped to his mother, a chord I knew I would cut.

A flock of migrating birds swarmed overhead
as I cherished the gurgling innocent in awkward arms

and my ache for distant Yorubaland began to haunt.
Joana wanted the fruits of love: sliced, scooped, mashed,

but I dared not know my hunger for fear I'd starve forever.
I needed a boy child. Her swollen womb bore me one.

I let Joana have him for twelve good years. In the thirteenth
a ship was loading in the bay to take emancipados to Africa.

She was hysterical. 'I'll *never* leave Bahia. It's my home!'
You'll never take my son away, Nunca! Nunca! Nunca!'

'The boy will decide. He is old enough.'
I said, 'Gregorio, my son, you are of the Yoruba tribe.

Your forefathers came here as slaves many years ago.
I have saved enough money to cross the Atlantic.

Will you travel with me and live as a free man,
or will you always be underdog to the white man in Brazil?

He answered, clear-eyed and sure, 'I will sail with you, Baba.'
I cried. The year – 1875 – we went home.

BABA

WAS THIS the land of my great–grandmother home?
This strange island of swirling cloth and colour clash?

I found these people so arrogant, quarrelsome, so proud.
Years later I realised we enslaved had been subdued,

by then my stride had the measure of ownership too.
We Brazilians were plenty, were prosperous, ambitious.

I became a master at the first Portuguese school,
like an uprooted seed in time my roots took hold.

When they finally stopped slavery, more Brazilians
sought harbour in Lagos. We welcomed them.

None had any news of Joana. Is she alive today?
I only know that her tears, like a curse, still damn me.

Ha! My memories are a fort in which I am the prisoner.

> Baba opened his mouth to speak, but ghosts flew out.
> The muscled baobab leaves whispered behind him.
>
> Taiwo sat dazed and speechless in the bristling silence.
> He crept off into twilight, a cat courting the shadows.
>
> Baba would sit up by the light of a kerosene lamp.
> The world he entered Taiwo would never know.

CHAPTER 20

Lagos, Nigeria, 1946 –

SHAKESPEARE, Keats, Socrates and the Romans'
ink ran like Greek messengers across golden sands

in the class books for boys at King's College, Lagos,
where beneath the whizz of a whirring fan, Taiwo's keen

brain processed words that would shape his vision,
his fountain pen poised for Imperial College, London.

Immersed in the soliloquy of Lear's madness,
Taiwo found no time for his grandfather's reminiscences,

now bloated beyond walking with elephantiasis legs,
his thickened skin tended by maids and Zenobia;

while Gregorio was driven between cities on business,
had mistresses in the Cameroon, Togo, the Gold Coast;

and the day Baba left his body in his bed,
High Mass was said by the padre in Holy Cross Church,

the road closed for ceremonies – drummers, wailers, food,
while his body lay hollowed in his darkened bedroom.

His secret idols lit by candles, the stone altar in the wall,
Baba's journey had begun.

GOURD-BELLIED, guava-sweet, crisp as custard apple,
Kehinde seeded a child soon after marriage to Segun,

kept Zenobia company while Segun studied Britain's law
and Gregorio's absences rumoured a new wife in Warri.

Kehinde teased Taiwo daily over his self-conscious strut,
badgered him on the steps as the island's sun sagged,

splashing zinc roofs rust, whitewashed walls dusty pink.
Their mama sneaked out, whacked Taiwo's growing head,

to show him he was no man *yet* and still her baby boy.
He leaned on the balcony, recited Shelley's olde verses,

as Kehinde rolled her eyes at his clipped British tones,
yawned dramatically when he rambled on about rolling

Yorkshire moors, King George, Big Ben, cream teas,
Christmas trees and, unbelievably, *snow*. How he'd stroll

through the City with bowler and brolly, amble into a pub
'A pint of ale, my man!' white froth fringing his top lip.

'I say, what a lovely day!' Taiwo swung from pillar
to pillar on the white parapet, bellowed to bemused

neighbours as they passed in Ibosere Road below.
Rosy-cheeked milkmaids obsessed his nights. Pale thighs.

Pink nipples. *Pink* nipples! His member burst with excitement.
Great Britain. The United Kingdom. The Motherland.

SOMETIMES a child drowns in a storm drain
or a body is fished out of the lagoon; palm oil, coins,

cock's blood and secrets in a calabash by a crossing
meant Hubert Soglo of Dahomey was commissioned.

As the foetus in Kehinde invaded, nightmares descended.
She saw buildings collapse into rubble and dust,

her father in a tumultuous sea, arms flailing, her unborn
entombed for eternity in her womb, with the face

of Baba, his voice pleading, 'It – is – not – time – yet.'
Those mornings when she battled to banish

her night foes, she awoke shaking. Sensing,
her mama rushed in with a damp cloth,

lay her daughter's head on her lap, eased her frown
out from forehead to crown, becalmed her.

News spread through the city, flames reached Zenobia
that the wandering Gregorio had been waylaid by robbers

on the road to Badagry, and before the hour was out,
the whole island knew of his mutilation by cutlass.

> Zenobia was used to the sunken space his side of the bed.
> 'Life's so hard,' she thought. He had provided, but his love?

> The kernel of a bitter kola nut. She never knew him.
> At the burial she wailed but did not mourn her husband.

She stood there in her best blue wrapper and head-tie,
the silent Zenobia, and the sea poured out of her.

She stood there until the ship had pulled out of harbour,
out of sight. Still, she stood there, listening

to the waves against the harbour walls. She looked out
onto the Slave Coast, Bight of Benin, the Atlantic

which had brought Gregorio from Brazil, and Baba.
Forever she stood there, watched the clouds converge,

prayed that her boy Taiwo would be safe on his journey,
happy in his new home. She thought of her marriage

without love, her childhood home in Abeokuta, Kehinde
about to give birth, and Baba – who was watching her now.

And she did not feel the salt sea stream down her face,
did not feel the steady breeze blow in from parts

of the world she would never know; and when the stars
appeared in the deepening sky, she felt a tug at her arm,

it was Kehinde, come to lead her from that place
which gave life, took life, and she knew with a mother's love

that the sea would not bring her son back.

EPILOGUE

Rio de Janeiro, Brazil, 1995

LARA

CORCOVADO, Christ the Redeemer, holds flirty Rio
in its outstretched arm-span, beneficent padre, 700 metres

up canopied mountain. I hike the forested incline
to awe at its monolithic pleated hem, marvel at Rio,

lushly subdued, panoramically shimmering beneath me.
I feel its blank stone eyes follow me in this sexing city

of beached homens with corrugated stomachs, g-string
bonitas with football-hard buttocks, hoovered cellulite.

With my camel-hump rucksack and grunge-green shorts
I feel like a poor relation in this glamorous metropolis,

yet the favela shacks, masses of tumbledown boxes,
are homes for the disempowered, make picturesque hills

from afar for the muitos cruzeiros who stroll the laundered
beaches of Ipanema and Copacabana at sundown.

Escaping Rio, the bus to Bahia spirals mountain precipices,
vertiginous facades lubricated by gushing springs which spurt

out of nowhere. Come dawn we speed past dehydrated
horizons spiked with cacti like three-pronged forks.

My swollen feet tingle as we decelerate into Salvador,
where I hope the past will close in on me.

SALVADOR grips its Yoruba mother like a shawl,
threadbare, tattered at the ends, yet refusing to yield

to wind, fly back over the Atlantico to home.
Bahianas in white sizzle acarajé from stools, as if no sea

no history separates them from the traders of Lagos.
Resting in a high-panelled room in Terreiro de Jesus,

I hear the wheels of the barrow boys on its cobbles,
imagine carriages clobbering its enslaved streets.

Yoruba words sign buildings, pepper Portuguese,
its deities re-located in Candomblé; when bloco bands

converge drumming on Praça da Se, I feel the blood
of war pass into my soul, thrilling me. Rastas and hippies

carve orixas in doorways, busk, sell artefacts on mats.
Entering the Afro-Brasileiro museum I secretly hope

for a clue, a photograph of a great-grandfather or mother,
whom I will somehow instantly, miraculously recognise.

'Any da Costas still around?' I ask the attendant.
'Of course. Hundreds. Thousands. Hundreds of thousands.'

I leave the city of passion for the port of Belem,
not knowing what to look for anymore.

I CROSS the state line into Amazon country at 4 A.M.,
turfed out of my seat to show proof of a yellow fever jab.

Belem is a pasty-faced city that sells hammocks.
I buy one. Take the first boat out down the Amazon,

to reflect, to dream. I string my stripy bedfellow
on deck, intimately close to others, returnees, mostly.

I shower in brown river water, stuff banana sarnies,
avoid a blocked-up loo, and for the next fortnight

I watch the jungle fill me up as the boat slices
through melted chocolate, its engine, my heart, synchronised.

We move on into solitude. My thoughts become free
of the chaos of the city, uncensored, the river calms me.

I become my parents, my ancestors, my gods. We dock,
a remote settlement. I stretch my pins, earthed, follow

my singing ears, Catholic hymns hybridised by drums.
A hilltop church, Indian congregation, holding

palm fronds. It is Palm Sunday. I hum from the door,
witness to one culture being orchestrated by another.

The past is gone, the future means transformation.
The boat's horn impatiently calls me. I panic away.

To the riverbank, the jungle, the contemplation.

A RAINSTORM hammers Manaus, rivering streets.
I emerge onto concrete, wobbly, the quayside spinning,

my heart replete with time and hope; I locate a Chinese
eaterie, replenish my banana self on noodles,

await the dazzling sun to rainbow the Amazon sky
magical again. When the downpour abates, I head

for the waterfall at Cachoera do Taruma, descend
its slippery slopes, strip off, revitalised by icy cascades.

I am baptised, resolved to paint slavery out of me,
the Daddy People onto canvas with colour-rich strokes.

Their songs will guide me in sweaty dreams at night.
I savour living in the world, planet of growth, of decay,

think of my island, the 'Great' Tippexed out of it,
tiny amid massive floating continents, the African one

an embryo within me. I will wing back to Nigeria
again and again, excitedly swoop over a zigzag

of amber lights signalling the higgledy energy of Lagos.
                              It is time to leave.

Back to London, across international time zones.
I step out of Heathrow and into my future.

GLOSSARY

Some of the Brazilian/Portuguese words are Yoruba. All the
names of the gods are Yoruba words which have different spelling
in Brazil, for example, *orisha* in Yoruba becomes orixa in Brazil.
Brazilian words with the letter 'x' are pronounced 'sh'. Yoruba
words with the letter 's' are pronounced 'sh'.

Acaraje	Fried bean cake
Adiré	Blue patterned cloth
Africanos livres	Free Africans
Agbada	Traditional Yoruba gown (male)
Aguda	Freed Brazilian slave in Nigeria
Seanathair	grandfather
Baba	Father, term of respect for an elder
Babalao	High priest of Candomblé
Bandeirante	Members of early mission to open up interior of Brazil. They often waged war with the quilombos
Berimbau	Stringed musical instrument
Bloco	Large carnival drumming group
Bonita	Pretty
Branco	White
Buba	Female blouse
Cabo Sile	Hail the King
Cachaça	Sugar cane rum
Candomblé	Afro-Brazilian religion
Cruzeiro	Brazilian currency
Daidí	Daddy
Dodo	Plantain
Egun	Spirits of the dead who participate in Voudon rites
Eleggua	God of the Crossroads
Escravos	Slaves
Favela	Shanty town, slum
Fazenda	Large plantation
Fuji	Modern type of Nigerian music
Gelé	Yoruba headtie
Homens	Men

Iro	Mother
Juju	Magic, supernatural powers
Omole	Drums (tom-tom)
Ogun	God of Warriors (and iron tools/weapons)
Orixas	Yoruba gods
Oxala	Lord of Creation, greatest of the orixas
Oxumare	Hermaphrodite God of the Rainbow
Mamaí	mummy
Mamó	grandmother
Moreno	Skin tone between black and white
Muitos	Many
Nunca	Never
Quilombo	Organised community of escaped Africans who lived independently of slavery, usually in the hills. The largest was Palmares which numbered 30,000 people
Sarara	Freckled mulatto with blue/green eyes
Sasanach	Englishman
Talibi	Yoruba name for a child who is born with head and body covered with a caul
Xango	God of Thunder and Lightning

ACKNOWLEDGEMENTS

Special thanks are due to Neil Astley, my editor at Bloodaxe Books, for his prodigious commitment to poetry and to this book. To my early reader, the poet Kwame Dawes, who gave important feedback on an earlier incarnation of this book; and to my later reader and husband David, for spending hours going over this manuscript with his blue pen when he could have been watching *The Sopranos* instead.